LOST IN THE LIGHTS

Other books by Paul Hemphill

NONFICTION
The Ballad of Little River
Wheels
The Heart of the Game
Leaving Birmingham
Me and the Boy
Too Old to Cry
The Good Old Boys
The Nashville Sound

FICTION
Nobody's Hero
King of the Road
The Sixkiller Chronicles
Long Gone

COLLABORATIONS
Climbing Jacob's Ladder (with Jock M. Smith)
Mayor (with Ivan Allen Jr.)

LOST IN THE LIGHTS

Sports, Dreams, and Life

PAUL HEMPHILL

The University of Alabama Press
Tuscaloosa and London

Copyright © 2003 The University of Alabama Press
All rights reserved
The University of Alabama Press
Tuscaloosa, Alabama 35487–0380
Manufactured in the United States of America

Designer: Michele Myatt Quinn
Typeface: Minion

∞

The paper on which this book is printed meets the minimum
requirements of American National Standard for Information
Science–Permanence of Paper for Printed Library Materials,
ANSI Z39.48-1984.

Library of Congress Cataloging-in-Publication Data

Hemphill, Paul, 1936–
    Lost in the lights: sports, dreams, and life / by Paul Hemphill.
      p.   cm.
    ISBN 0-8173-1316-8 (pbk. : alk. paper)
      1. Sports stories, American. 2. Southern States—Fiction. 3.
Southern States—Social life and customs. I. Title.

PS3558.E4793 L67 2003
813'.54—dc21   2002151265

British Library Cataloguing-in-Publication Data available

In Memory of Dick Schaap

Contents

LOST IN THE LIGHTS

Prologue

FOR MANY MALES OF MY generation who would turn out to be writers, this is a familiar tale. We grew up wanting to become athletes, but then, having failed, we opted for writing about sports. In my case, as you shall see, the dream was to become a major-league second baseman. I was stopped in my tracks early on, being cut after less than a week in spring training with a woeful minor-league club, a failure at the age of eighteen, and only then did I begin to consider any sort of life beyond baseball. That led to college, which led to a kindly English professor at Auburn who opined that I seemed to have "a way with words." Thus emboldened, told for the first time that there was something I might be good at, I rushed out and bought a flimsy little portable typewriter and became a writing fool. I taught myself how to type and how to write. *Write what you know* was the mantra then, as now, and since I had read more of *The Sporting News* than of Shakespeare, I chose sportswriting. Soon I became sports editor of my college newspaper, the very year that Auburn's football team won the national championship, and that led to a half-dozen years of writing about sports for daily newspapers in medium-sized Southern cities.

But as I grew up and out, reading serious literature and having serious thoughts for the first time, I developed the notion that writing about sports was child's play, a painless way to make a living, something we do before graduating to *real* writing. Somewhere in that period I came across a collection of pieces by Paul Gallico, wherein he recounted the precise moment when he decided to quit his job on a New York newspaper, as the highest-paid sports columnist in America, in order to address "the real world." It was a Sunday afternoon and, faced with having to crank out a 1,000-word column by sundown, he got off the elevator only to be greeted by a hairy cigar-smoking pressroom foreman: "Well, Gallico, is that crap of yours gonna be late again tonight?" That about did it. Gallico marched straight to his typewriter, knocked out an essay entitled "Farewell to Sport," quit his job, and nearly starved until he got the hang of writing without using sports as a safety net. Such novels as *The Snow Goose* and *Mrs. 'arris Goes to Paris* would follow, but in the end he would admit, as we all do, that writing every day in the service of the Toys & Games Department had been the perfect preparation— boot camp, as it were—for everything he would write afterward. After all, the only people on a newspaper who are allowed to actually *write* are the sportswriters, who are given free rein to describe scenes and quote dialogue and dramatize action and, as a New York sports editor once famously said, "tell us how the weather was." All of this was a variation on something Ernest Hemingway once said of newspapering in general: "On the Kansas City *Star* you were taught to write a simple declarative sentence. This cannot be harmful to anyone. The trick is to know when to quit."

What came after those early days of writing sports for newspapers was what I call a natural progression. I had spent my time in boot camp as a sports editor and columnist in such outposts as Augusta, Georgia, and Tampa, Florida, and I knew only that I'd had enough of writing about sports on a daily basis. I had done my time. What might follow I didn't know until somewhere around 1963 when I came upon the New York *Herald-Tribune* and saw that Jimmy Breslin, who had produced a hilarious book about the original New York Mets entitled *Can't Anybody Here Play This Game?*, had moved over from the sports page to write a general column in what today's papers would call the Style section. Instead of writing about athletes, the new and reconstituted

Breslin was taking to the streets to write these marvelous portraits of bartenders, construction workers, cops, floozies, bookies, and housewives—regular people making it through their days—in taut narrative scenes that read like Updikian short stories. They were shorter versions of what Joseph Mitchell had been writing for years in the gleaming pages of *The New Yorker.* Jimmy's work, like that of Gay Talese and Tom Wolfe in longer forms, was being hailed as the New Journalism. *The man's writing literature,* I thought. *In a newspaper.* For me, it was bye-bye to sport.

Within a year or so of discovering Breslin's column, I found myself doing the same thing in Atlanta, for the afternoon *Journal.* Six times a week, in sickness or in health, I had to hit the pavement and produce these little 1,000-word human dramas to "feed the monster," as an old guy on the city desk once said of newspapering, and after more than four years and 1.2 million words I was burned out, emotionally and physically. The next step, in the natural progression of a writer's development, was to free-lance magazine work. I was writing for all of them, it seemed—*Life, TV Guide, Cosmopolitan, Sport, True, Atlantic Monthly, The New York Times Sunday Magazine,* et al.—trading the twenty-four-hour shelf life of a newspaper for the slightly longer life of a magazine. Soon that became unsatisfying, and I began writing nonfiction books. And finally, like most writers, I took the next logical step: writing the sainted novel. The progression seemed complete. Now, being of reasonably sound mind and body in my mid-sixties, I reckon that I've had more than four million words published in forms up to and including books. It's been a long march from those days when I wrote sports for newspapers and magazines.

Because I'd been in denial for so long about my sportswriting, still promising that I was going to stop as soon as I could shake the habit, I first took it as an affront when asked if I'd like to put together a collection of my sports pieces for this book. My argument, mostly to myself, was that I've written books about a lot of things beyond sports: the sad story of a racially inspired church arson in rural Alabama, a memoir of growing up in a hostile Birmingham, the tale of a fitful hike of the Appalachian Trail with my estranged teenaged son, a report on "the Nashville Sound" that was said to be less about country music than a commentary on the evolution of the South, collaborations with a heroic ex-mayor of Atlanta and a colorful black attorney from Tuskegee, and a novel based on my truck-driving father.

But then I got to taking a closer look at my career as I pored through my books and boxes of stuff, and it didn't take long to realize that the joke's on me. Maybe I can't help myself, I don't know; once a sportswriter, always a sportswriter. Of my eleven nonfiction books, including this one, three are purely about sports and two of the general collections are heavy with sports profiles. Of my four novels, two are drawn on a sports canvas. Even the novel I find myself working on today is about baseball, in its own peculiar way (see "The Kid and the Third Baseman" in these pages for the genesis), although it is *really* about a lot of other things, including anti-Semitism and the effects of the Second World War on America. Make of it what you will. A friend of mine—and only a friend could get away with this—said to me, after the publication of *Wheels*, "Okay. Books about country music, truck-driving, and stock-car racing. What's next, now that you've completed your Bubba Trilogy?" All I could say was, putting on my professor's tweed jacket, *Hey, you write what you know.*

By that time, I had finally made a separate peace with myself. What I knew was that writers of every ilk choose the canvas they're most comfortable with to deliver their message. For Breslin, it's the streets of New York. For John Steinbeck, it was the downtrodden Okies and *paisanos* who had somehow drifted to California. For Hemingway, it was any place where a man might test his mettle under pressure. William Faulkner and Eudora Welty had their rural Mississippi, John Updike his small-town mid-Atlantic, Erskine Caldwell his Southern textile villages, Raymond Chandler his seedy downtown Los Angeles. The key in every case is that they found the world they knew best, their canvas, and decided early on that there is where they would paint.

The basics of life—joys and sorrows, victories and defeats—are found wherever you look, and they are as real for a Philadelphia socialite as for a sawmill yahoo or a semiliterate grandson of slaves in the Black Belt of Alabama. Once I understood that, I settled on sports and the bluecollar South, often using both at the same time, as my canvases. "It don't matter where you cut it at," the country singer Merle Haggard once told me, of why he made his records in California rather than in Nashville. "It's what you put in the groove."

During the 'seventies I certainly wrote my share of magazine articles that hardly rose above the level of pure sports pieces intended for avid fans. Most of them were written for *Sport* magazine, which I had eagerly read as a teenager, profiles on such heroes as Ernie Banks, Oscar Robertson, Dale Murphy, and the like. This was during my period of denying that I was just another sportswriter. But it was fun, just the same, especially with Dick Schaap as editor. Dick would say he wanted me to go to Tulsa and do a piece about a black basketball player named Richard Fuqua, then leading the nation in scoring for, of all places, Oral Roberts University. "I don't care what you write," he said, "but I've already got the headline. 'Praise the Lord and Pass the Ball to Fuqua.'" He wanted me to fly to the Dominican Republic and track down Rico Carty, rehabilitating a damaged knee during the off-season, but I couldn't flush out "Beeg Boy" with a series of letters, wires, and phone calls. "Just get on a plane and go down there," Schaap said. "He's a national treasure. He couldn't hide if he wanted to." Schaap was a national treasure himself when he died unexpectedly last year: co-author of dozens of sports autobiographies, a familiar interviewer on ESPN, perhaps the most knowledgeable sports reporter on the American scene.

But those pieces got me out of the house, paid some bills, and are not represented here. Not surprisingly, having had my say about how some sportswriting can transcend sports if you do it right, I respectfully submit that this collection is not a sports book. Schaap was always looking for pieces that would dig deeper than that, and a couple I wrote for him appear here: my boyhood infatuation with the minor-league Birmingham Barons, and the sad end of a former All-American football player named Bob Suffridge. The one is about childhood innocence, the other about a lion in winter, both set to the music of sports. That's what I was looking for as I set to winnowing the list down to a workable size. I wanted timeless themes as I went about the selection process; pieces that transcend sport; pieces that ultimately deal not so much with sport but with life; pieces that will live beyond next year's pennant race.

The title, *Lost in the Lights,* is not only a play on a baseball alibi ("Aw, hell, I lost it in the lights") but a metaphor as well—the "lights" being the spotlight under which most athletes live and perform. Random as the selections might seem at first to be, they were carefully chosen to represent the different stages of a man's life. Thus, in Part I, "The Dawning," we have pieces that essentially deal with boys hoping to become men. In Part II, "The Striving," we see men at work, however disparate those labors. And in Part III, "The Gloaming," there are glimpses of twilight, the time of broken dreams, my lions in winter. Some may call it sport. I call it life.

PART ONE The Dawning

White Bread and Baseball

IT WAS ENOUGH TO MAKE a man cry. In another time, during the years immediately following the end of the Second World War, there would have been a jaunty mob of some four hundred red-faced steelworkers and truck drivers and railroad switchmen lined up at the four ticket windows—the soot and grease of a day's work still smeared on their bodies, their eyes darting as they waited to get inside old Rickwood Field to take out their frustrations on the hated Atlanta Crackers—but now, hardly an hour before a game between the Birmingham A's and the Jacksonville Suns, the place was like a museum. Five rheumy old-timers lolled about the one gate that would be open for the night. A cadaverous old fellow who had celebrated his eighty-second birthday the night before sat on a stool in the lobby behind a podium stacked with scorecards, a position he had occupied for most of this century, calling out "Scorecards, get your scorecards!" in the same froggy voice I remember from the first day I walked through these turnstiles twenty-seven years ago, in 1947. On the cracked plaster wall, needing a dusting, were the familiar faded photographs of the heroes of my youth: Fred Hatfield, Walt Dropo, Eddie Lyons, Red Mathis, Jimmy Piersall, Mickey Rutner, and, not the least, a rabbit-quick drag-bunting outfielder named Ralph "Country" Brown. In contrast to the 1948 season, when the Birmingham Barons of the Class AA Southern Association averaged more than 7,000 paid fans per game, the attendance on this blustery June night in 1974 would come to exactly 338.

Mounting the creaky stairs to the executive offices, I sought out an old acquaintance. Glynn West had been fifteen years old in '48, the holder of an exalted position in the eyes of the rest of us. On summer afternoons when the Barons were playing at home he walked the two miles from his apartment project to operate the scoreboard and supervise the younger kids lucky enough to be hired to shag baseballs hit out of the park during batting practice. Now, in his forties, he found himself general manager of a totally different Birmingham club, no longer called the Barons, fuzzy-cheeked chattels of the Oakland A's farm system.

Seated behind a desk adorned with historic baseballs and photographs from the glory days, West wasn't angry at anybody. "We used to get free publicity on the radio and in the papers," he was saying. "It was a civic responsibility to support the home team back then. But last year we had to spend as much as we spent in an entire three-year period in the late 1940s just to draw twenty thousand people against the million we drew in 1948, '49, and '50."

"Doesn't anybody care?"

"Oakland cares to the extent that every dollar we take in means a dollar they don't have to pay out. They'll call and say, 'Sorry, Glynn, but we've got to take so-and-so from you. We're calling him up to the big club.' What can I say? If it wasn't for Oakland, I guess we wouldn't have a club in the first place. When we were kids and some rain would come up, the fans would jump out of the stands to help spread the tarpaulin on the field. Now only one club in the league even has a tarp. We had to sell ours to help pay some bills." He fiddled with a baseball once signed by a great Barons team of the past. "Go find a seat if you want to. There's plenty for everybody. Last year we had a promotion where the first one hundred people through the gate got a free copy of *The Sporting News*. Four people went away mad."

The Birmingham Barons. With the possible exception of the one week I spent in the spring training camp of a grubby Class D club in the Florida Panhandle during the mid-1950s, no experience in my life has been so profound as my undying awe for the hundreds of fading outfielders and flame-throwing young pitchers and haggard managers who wore the uniform of the Barons during the late '40s and early '50s. It began on a Sunday in late August of '47 when my old man, a long-distance truck driver, announced that we were going to see my first professional baseball game. The Barons, stumbling along then as threadbare members of the old Philadelphia Athletics farm system, were playing a doubleheader against the strong Dodgers-operated Mobile Bears at Rickwood. I fell in love with it all that day, at eleven years of age, the moment we walked up a ramp and I saw the bright sun flashing on the manicured grass and the gaudy billboarded outfield fence and the flashing scoreboard in left-center and the tall silver girders supporting the lights. I would later read that Rickwood was regarded as one of the finest parks in the minor leagues, but nobody had to tell me that. Yankee Stadium would not have been more impressive to me. Taking our seats, we became one with the crowd: hooting at the umpires, needling the opposition, scrambling for foul balls hit into the stands, *ooh*-ing when a lanky Mobile first baseman named Chuck Connors towered a home run all the way over the right-field roof (*the* Chuck Connors, later famous as "The Rifleman" of the television series). Only the mighty Ted Williams had ever done that before, my old man advised me. The Barons lost both games that day, the second game shortened when disgusted fans began sailing their rented seat cushions onto the field at dusk, and I even found that exciting, assuming it was the norm.

From that day on and for the next ten years Rickwood and the Barons were at the center of my life. Hurrying to deliver my seventy-eight copies of the afternoon Birmingham *News* (after first reading sports editor Zipp Newman's account of the Barons game of the night before), I would take the one-hour trolley ride to Rickwood in hopes of arriving early enough to see the players crunch into the gravel parking lot around five o'clock before suiting up and heading onto the field for batting practice. (Once I was stunned to see that a particular favorite was a gaunt chain-smoker.) In those days the big-league clubs played their way up from Florida to begin the regular season, and during one spring exhibition game between the Barons and the Red Sox I out-scrambled an old geezer for a ball fouled into the bleachers by Walt Dropo, one of my heroes from the previous Barons team, who was getting his shot in the big leagues. It was a ball that we kids in my neighborhood were able to keep in play for the entire summer—my "Baron ball," repeatedly patched with waxed kite string until it finally wore out. At night when the Barons were playing on the road I would curl up in bed with the lights out and my radio under the covers to hear Gabby Bell's imaginative re-creation of the game, not knowing for some time that Gabby wasn't actually in, say, Nashville, but was sitting in a downtown studio with a "crowd machine" and constructing his "live" account from a Western Union ticker tape. Occasionally my family would load up the car at dawn with fried chicken and potato salad and tea and watermelon and ride to Atlanta or Memphis or Chattanooga to root the Barons through a Sunday doubleheader in the lair of the enemy. We always bought box seats next to the Barons' dugout. One time, in Memphis, Barons pitcher Willard Nixon gave me a baseball at day's end because I was the most vociferous Barons fan in the ballpark that day, and I curled up with it in the back seat of the car during the long drive home that night.

Nor did the interest wane during the off-season. There was always some Barons news in the Birmingham papers every day of the fall and winter: the Barons had renewed their spring-training lease in Ocala, Florida; or they had signed a fading major leaguer such as Brooklyn's Marv Rackley or the Senators' Bobo Newsom; or they had sold a star from the previous season to a big-league club and he was "thankful for the wonderful fans in Birmingham." And then there was the Hot Stove League. Every Monday night in January and February, downtown at the Thomas Jefferson Hotel, a covey of locally-bred stars like Dixie and Harry Walker and Alex and Pete Grammas and Jimmy and Bobby Bragan would lollygag with fans and then watch a black-and-white film of the most recent World Series, narrated by Mel Allen. And, too, you were likely to run into a Baron star on the streets in December—Eddie Lyons riding shotgun in an ambulance, Fred

Hatfield selling suits in the men's department at Blach's department store, Norm Zauchin operating a bowling alley—for these were the days when a player might settle down with one minor-league club during the remaining years of his career.

Looking back, I'm still convinced that during those years the Southern Association was the best all-around minor league in the history of baseball. The eight cities were paired off in four perfectly natural civic rivalries—Atlanta and Birmingham, Little Rock and Memphis, Nashville and Chattanooga, Mobile and New Orleans—and it was, indeed, regarded as one's civic responsibility to support the home team. Twice my old man and I stood for five hours behind a rope in center field with two thousand others (Rickwood seated 16,000 then) to shout obscenities at the Atlanta Crackers during Sunday doubleheaders. The nearest major-league operations were the Washington Senators and the St. Louis Cardinals. All of the clubs in the Southern Association had strong working agreements with big-league organizations, but they also had a certain amount of financial autonomy. After one particularly successful season, the general manager of the Barons, a feisty Philadelphia Irishman named Eddie Glennon, magnanimously sent a check for $5,000 to millionaire Red Sox owner Tom Yawkey "in appreciation for what the Boston Red Sox organization did" to help the Barons.

There simply wasn't anything better to do during summer nights in those Southern cities at that time. There was no air conditioning, and television hadn't quite come into its own. There were no nightclubs, thanks to the hard-shell Baptists, and there was scant affluence to create the disposable income necessary to spread the joys of boating, golf, and expensive dining to the masses. And so, in Birmingham and Chattanooga and those other bleak workingman's towns of the postwar South, baseball was the only game in town. Fans passed the hat around the box seats after a meaningful performance to show their appreciation in dollars and cents. Businesses offered free suits or radios or hundred-dollar bills for home runs or shutouts or game-winning hits. Kids, like young Paul Hemphill, went speechless in the presence of Fred Hatfield. Citizens offered the use of their garage apartments, rent-free, to whoever happened to be the Barons' shortstop that year. In this atmosphere the Barons of 1948, with 445,926 paid customers and a total attendance of some 510,000 for seventy home dates, outdrew the St. Louis Browns of the American League.

With infield practice over, Harry Bright stood smoking a cigarette in the runway leading from the playing field to the newly remodeled A's clubhouse while his young players changed sweatshirts and relieved bladders and played fast games of poker. Bright is forty-five now, a baseball itinerant since the day he signed a contract with the Yankees at the age of sixteen. He knocked around the minor leagues for twelve years, hitting .413 one year in the woolly West Texas–New Mexico League, before getting in eight big-league seasons as a utility player. This was his ninth season as a minor-league manager, his second straight with Birmingham. I remembered when he played for a great Memphis Chicks team in the early 1950s, a club managed by Luke Appling and stocked with several veterans who had leveled off at Class AA.

"Yeah, that was in '53," he was saying, leaning against a concrete wall in a gold-and-green uniform identical to that of the parent Oakland A's. "I was making $350 a month."

"How'd you feed your family?"

"With a lot of peanut butter."

He flipped the cigarette away. "Actually, I picked up a lot on the side that year. You remember that laundry that used to pay $200 for every home run hit by a Memphis Chick?"

"Sure," I said. "Memphis Steam Laundry."

"Right."

"Had their plant behind the center-field fence."

"Right. Well," said Bright, "I hit fifteen homers that year and fourteen of 'em were at home. Somebody said the laundry shelled out $21,000 in home run money that year. We had a lot of power."

Bright's eyes would shine as the old names and stories were brought up. Ted Kluszewski, Jimmy Piersall, Carl Sawatski. The train travel, the grotesque 257-foot right-field fence atop an embankment at Sulphur Dell in Nashville, the wild extravaganzas promoted by entrepreneur Joe Engel ("Barnum of the Bushes") in Chattanooga. The low pay, the poor lights, the fleabag hotels, the maniacal fans, the hopelessness of it all. But Harry Bright has, by necessity, quit living in the past. "It's my job now," he said, "to bring these kids along and prepare 'em for the big club. You know. Teach 'em the 'A's way of baseball.' It would be better for them if more people came out for the games, because a crowd gives you an edge, makes you go harder. But people won't buy minor-league baseball anymore. They can see the real thing, the big leagues, on television. What the hell." His club was slumping into last place. Bright pulled the lineup card from his hip pocket and trudged out to meet the umpires at home plate to go over the ground rules. Hardly anyone noticed.

I should have seen the first signs of demise as early as 1950 when my mother came to see my YMCA team play on a rocky grade-school sandlot one day and commented afterward that she would rather watch "boys I know" than go to Rickwood to witness "boys from Chicago and places like that," no matter how good the latter were. When the Little League program came along, involving every kid in America with any propensity for the game at all, it robbed the minor leagues of the business from those kids' parents. Those parents were the hardest of the hard-core fans. Then along came television and air conditioning and affluence (and then the Atlanta Braves, in the case of the Deep South), and one day the minor leagues simply died in their sleep.

The state of Georgia once had twenty-two minor-league towns; now, in 1974, it had only three. In 1973, the Southern Association as a whole drew two thousand fewer fans than Birmingham alone had drawn in 1948. During this season of '74 there is no radio broadcast of Birmingham A's games, and the baseball writer for the morning paper is the thirteen-year-old son of the sports editor of the *Post-Herald*. Rickwood Field is as pretty as ever, although some of the uncovered bleachers have been taken down. These were once called the "nigger bleachers," and it was below them that a precocious teenager named Willie Mays once made incredible catches for the Birmingham Black Barons of the Negro American League before baseball finally desegregated. Now high school football and baseball games share billing with the A's on the lush green turf of Rickwood where once Eddie Lyons and Walt Dropo and Gus Triandos and Country Brown and hundreds of my other childhood heroes romped and stirred my heart.

One of the most prominent billboards lining the outfield fences at Rickwood these days is one reading "When Visiting Atlanta See the Braves." As the game went on that night, Harold Seiler squinted in that direction and tugged at his A's cap and patted the knee of his wife, Mabel, sitting beside him in their third-base box seats, not knowing quite what he could add to the story of the death of the Birmingham Barons. Hal Seiler owns a paint store in Birmingham and has been known, for as long as anybody can remember, as the city's Number One Baron booster. Nearly every night of a Birmingham home game for some three decades, he and his wife have been there. One night last year, in fact, he suited up and actually managed the A's through one of those insufferable late-season "let's-get-it-over-and-go-home" exercises.

"Coached third, even changed a pitcher," he said.

"You win?"

"Won it, four-to-one. Bright panicked and took his job back."

Minnie Minoso's son, a good-looking Kansas City prospect playing right field for Jacksonville, cut down a runner trying to go from first to third and got applause from the Seilers. A black man in the grandstand behind Seiler suddenly broke out into a funky dance in the aisle, wildly thrashing about in a cream-colored suit. "Name's 'Cat.' Comes every night, too, wearing a different outfit every time. Hell, I bet I know the first name of two hundred of these people here tonight. It's like a family reunion out here."

"Zeb Eaton," I said. "You remember Zeb Eaton?"

"Sure, the one that got beaned."

"What year?" We were playing Barons trivia now.

"Nineteen and forty-seven."

"You were here?"

"Me, at Rickwood? I was always here."

"Eaton," I said. "Hell of a prospect."

"Me and Mabel were right here. We heard the thud of the ball hitting his head. Ballpark sounded like a morgue. I helped pass the hat and raise money for Zeb's hospital bill. He was never the same after that."

I said, "Joe Scheldt. I bet you don't remember Joe Scheldt."

"Joe Scheldt?" Seiler was all smiles. "Crazy, absolutely bananas. Fast as a rabbit, though. Let me give *you* one. I remember all of 'em. Edo Vanni." I told him that I certainly did remember Edo Vanni, an outfielder who passed through briefly as a Baron, and Seiler was crestfallen. "I didn't know *anybody* remembered Edo Vanni," he said. "As a matter of fact, I didn't know anybody remembered the Barons." Just then, a pinch-hitter named Pickle Smith was announced for Jacksonville. "*Pickle!*" yelped Seiler. "*Pick*-le. Hey, that ain't no pickle, that's a *gherkin*. C'mon, you gherkin, back in the bottle." Smith stepped out of the batter's box and glared at Seiler. "Yeah, let's show the gherkin something out there." The last Birmingham Baron baseball fan, Harold Seiler, of Row Five, Box AA, Rickwood Field, smiled like a cherub as Pickle Smith struck out on three straight pitches.

Sport, 1974

2.

Big Night, Big City

THERE WERE A DOZEN of them, in identical blue blazers and gray slacks, and they hunched over on the eighth and ninth rows with their elbows on their knees and tried not to think about it. Their small blue overnight bags said "Crisp County High School Rebels" on the side. They could look on the floor and see Cedartown and Headland blurring up and down the polished court under the yellowish glare of the lights on the seventy-five-foot ceiling of the huge coliseum, the biggest coliseum any had ever thought he would see. They tried to keep their minds on the game, but they couldn't. One hour to go. All they could think about was the crowd and that huge floor and the smoke clinging to the ceiling.

Ben Rogers, their coach, sat ten rows behind them, studying the two teams on the floor. If Crisp won its nine o'clock game against Hart County, it would meet the winner of this one the next night. Rogers looked for weaknesses and strengths and it helped keep his mind off his own game.

"How are they?" somebody asked.

"Scared," Rogers said. "First night's always like this."

"How many have played here before?"

He thought for a minute. "Three. No, it's four. Four of 'em were with us when we came up last year."

"What'll you tell 'em?"

"What can you say? You just try to tell 'em it's no different from playing back home."

This was the first night, the opening round of the state Class AA high-school basketball tournament at Alexander Memorial Coliseum on the Georgia Tech campus. Sixteen teams from towns like Blue Ridge and Cedartown and Ringgold and Waycross. And Cordele, home of the Crisp County Rebels.

If you are accustomed to going by the coliseum every time Georgia Tech plays, and you are used to the lights and the crowds and the size of the place, it means nothing to you. It is the way basketball, big-time basketball, is played. But if you live on a farm like, say, Gib Williams does, this is it. This is the end of the line, the highest cloud. This is the place it led to, and this was the place it ended before you settled down and went to school and never again heard your name called out of a public-address system and had the people cheer for you all at the same time.

For Gib Williams, 6-foot-3, this was the big one. He was the starting center for the Crisp County Rebels. He lives on a farm outside Cordele. When he was cut from the squad before the 1965–66 season began, it was one of the worst things ever to happen to him. He fooled around with a basketball all summer and then gave up football so he could keep working through the fall. He wanted to make the basketball team. And he did. He was a substitute during the early games, and then he made the starting five, and now—on this night in the big city, Atlanta, 160 miles from Cordele—there was all of it boiling up inside him.

They were not talking. It was 8:30 and they were dressed now. Their ankles and wrists had been wrapped with white adhesive tape and they wore their gray warm-up jackets and they sat quietly in the dressing room, in the caverns of the coliseum. The dressing room was a small concrete cubicle, with gray steel lockers against the walls. Two bare light bulbs emitted a harsh light. Coach Ben Rogers stood next to the only door and looked up at them and they were all staring at the floor.

Rogers turned to the manager, a thin boy with a crew-cut. "How much time to play?"

"Three minutes, coach."

"Gib," Rogers said, "we've got to keep this Hill running. Wear him out."

Gib Williams nodded.

"This McCollum talks a lot," Rogers said. "He'll try to make you mad. Be sure you don't let him."

Nobody would so much as clear his throat. The tension had peaked out. If you swallow, everybody hears you. Rogers had to do something.

"There'll be more people out there than we ever saw."

Heads cropped.

"It's a big place. Bigger than any we've seen." It was wrong. Rogers knew it was wrong. He began walking from one end of the dressing room to the other. His heels clicked on the concrete. The manager came back in. He said there was two minutes' playing time left in the Headland-Cedartown game.

"Look," Rogers blurted, "it's no different than playing at West Crisp. Play it just like back home."

One of them yelled, "Don't give 'em nothing."

"Don't give 'em nothing but a hard time," said another.

Then Ben Rogers told them, softly, "Let's ease out of here."

The tension went quickly. There were the introductions. Then the tip-off. Hoke Hill, the gangly 6-6 center for Hart County, easily beat Gib Williams for the opening tip-off. It was 2–0, 2–2, 9–2, Hart, but by the end of the first quarter Crisp was ahead 14–12. Crisp still had the lead, 42–41, and was on the way to a big upset when the third quarter ended. But Hart's Alan Richardson found the range in the last period and Hart County burst ahead and won it, 67–58. For Gib Williams and his teammates, the ones he had practically lived with for all these months, it was over and the ramp to the dressing room seemed longer than before. And tomorrow morning, there would be 160 miles to cover between Atlanta and home.

Gib Williams wandered out of the dressing room. He had on his blazer and slacks now, and the blue overnight bag was dangling from one hand. Coach Rogers had told them they had done a good job and could hold their heads high, but that didn't help.

"You're a great basketball player," another player told Williams.

He mumbled thanks and walked down the hollow hallway.
"We did our best," he said.

"You gonna go to school, to college?"

"Probably to Cochran Junior College. Then Tech."

"Play basketball there?"

He said, "Naw, I don't think so."

"Scared tonight?"

"Yeah, plenty. You get used to it, but it scares you."

Maybe a hundred fans had come up from Cordele for the game. Gib Williams walked out of the narrow corridor leading from the dressing room and he saw his folks. His father is a lean, suntanned man, and his mother a pleasant housewife. His sister, a nurse in Atlanta, was with them.

"You boys did just wonderful," his mother said.

"I'm so sorry you lost," said his sister.

His father shook his hand. "Good job, son."

"Thanks. We tried." He looked at the floor.

"We're going to have to head back home," Mrs. Williams said.

"Okay."

"You want me to leave the car out for you, son?" she said.

"Uh-huh. Yes, ma'am."

"I'll see you Friday, Gib," his sister said.

"Yeah. Okay."

And that is how it ended. For Gib Williams, it is over. There will be other good days. There will be a wife, perhaps, and children. And business deals and vacations and grandchildren and better cars and a big house and moments that have big meanings. But they will be different. Nothing will ever be like it was last week, during March of 1967, when the Crisp County Rebels played for the state championship and over the public address system they were telling three thousand people, ". . . at center, number 50, Gib Williams. . . ."

Atlanta Journal, 1967

3

"I Gotta Let the Kid Go"

CRUISING THE BARREN STREETS one spring morning, eighteen years after the fact, I found it ludicrous that as a boy my life could have been rearranged in such a place; that I would still be haunted, all these years later, by a dream shattered in a town like Graceville, Florida. "Nobody ever stops here on purpose," I was once told, and although the judgment seemed a bit flippant—people do, after all, come from miles around on Sundays to eat fried shrimp at the Circle Grille—it had the ring of truth. Graceville (pop. 2,500) squats just inside the Florida line, in the company of Noma and Chipley and Two Egg, like a turtle broiling in the sun, the monotony of the oppressive Florida Panhandle broken only by occasional swirls of wind that lift the fine brown sand from the sidewalks and scatter it against the weathered frame buildings. Typical of most tiny Deep South farming communities, with their pickup trucks and feed stores and tattered storefront awnings under which leathery old white farmers share the shade with mute black laborers, Graceville is presided over by a bleak gray tin hulk identified on picture postcards as the World's Largest Peanut Sheller. Indeed, most of the changes that have taken place since the mid-1950s have been regressive. The movie house is closed now, leaving the Little Stag Pool Room as the center of entertainment, and to me there was a more poignant reminder of what had been lost: the sandwich-board sign that would have been propped up in the middle of the main intersection on another April morning—"BASEBALL TO-NITE, Oilers vs. Crestview, 7:30, Sportsman Park"—was there no more.

"Be right with you." Mike Tool was behind the counter at Cash Drugs, filling a vial with pills for a hunched old woman in a wilted cotton print dress and matching sunbonnet. When the Graceville Oilers were members of the Class D Alabama-Florida League during the 1950s, making Graceville the smallest town in professional baseball, Mike Tool was in charge of selling tickets and buying equipment and paying the players and handling anything else that came up. "Medicare day, busiest day of the month," he said when the woman had left. "Say you played for the Oilers?"

"In 1954. Spring of '54."

"Hemphill." He tried to remember. "There were so many."

"I didn't last but a week."

"Guess that explains it. Writer now, you say?"

"In Atlanta."

"Writer in *Atlanta*," he said, arching his eyebrows. "Lot of boys had to go to work. *Hard* work. Know what I mean? Bob Odenheimer, he works in a plant or something up in Illinois or Indiana. I forget which. Comes through just about every summer on vacation." Another customer was at the counter now, wanting a prescription filled. Tool flattened out the wrinkled scrap of paper, squinted to read the scrawl, then reached for a jug of capsules. "Sometimes," he said, "it's like the Oilers never happened."

Later, having driven across the railroad tracks to the ballpark, I waded through the weeds to where second base used to be and it started to come back: Joaquin Toyo chattering in broken English from shortstop, Al Rivenbark doing the splits at first base, manager Cat Milner drawling that all you had to do in baseball was "hit the ball and run like hell." Now the park lay like an abandoned farm. The light poles had been moved around for football, the rickety frame bus-shelter dugouts were gone, the tin left-field fence was buckling under kudzu, and the hand-painted letters reading SUPPORT GRACEVILLE OILERS BOOSTER CLUB were flaking off the concrete-block wall that had been our center-field fence. Even in its time it was one of the worst parks in organized baseball, and now it was a washed-up whore. What a place it had been, I thought, to join the company of men.

The game of baseball doesn't magnetize kids today as it did twenty-five years ago. Basically a measured and innocent diversion, baseball simply doesn't offer the pizzazz to grab a generation raised on color television and automobiles and weekends at the lake. The game hasn't changed, the kids have. Early on, they become sophisticated to a degree of cynicism that leaves no time for the unblinking worship of heroes that baseball always thrived upon. They play Little League ball, sure, but by the time they reach puberty they have had it all—the best equipment, manicured parks, their names in the papers, night games, crowds of one thousand—and there is no need to go on.

For those of us born during the Depression, however, it was an entirely different matter. Our pleasures were simple—double-dating on the trolley, roller skating, bowling, spending marathon Saturday mornings at the neighborhood "picture show" rooting for Hopalong Cassidy and the Green Hornet—and one of those pleasures was baseball. The game may never have it as good as it did in 1948, when five cities had at least two major-league teams (New York had three) and out across the land there were fifty-nine minor leagues, most of them in the South because of its warmer climate. Surrounded by baseball, we played it in the morning, watched it in the afternoon, and listened to it on radio at night.

I was fairly typical of my generation of Southerners, I suppose. I got hooked on the game when I heard Mel Allen's tense description of Enos ("Country") Slaughter of the Cardinals winning the '46 World Series over the Red Sox by scoring all the way from first base on a long single by Harry ("The Hat") Walker, who happened to be from Leeds, Alabama, not twenty miles east of where I was born. Baseball became my life one day the following spring when a young YMCA worker named Bill Legg came by the Minnie Holman Elementary School in Birmingham to give birth, amid cracked Arkansas Traveler bats and scarred baseballs and smelly sneakers, to the Woodlawn Blues.

Those were marvelously innocent times. Spring training began on Christmas Day, when my cousin and I gingered onto the vacant lot behind the fire station to try out our new spikes. By mid-January I was taking the trolley downtown to the Thomas Jefferson Hotel for the weekly Hot Stove League meeting in hopes of a glance at such local heroes as Red Mathis and Tommy O'Brien in their two-tone shoes and silk buttoned-at-the-neck sport shirts. And finally, the summer: hitching rides on the running board of Legg's Terraplane Hudson, playing games on rutted city playgrounds and schoolyards, replaying them over Coke floats at Hudson's Drug Store, catching my old man's pop flies until dark in the empty lot across from the house, stumping him with trivia from *The Sporting News* and *The Baseball Register* at suppertime, retiring to hear Gabby Bell's fanciful ticker-tape recreation of Birmingham Barons road games; papering the walls of my bedroom with full-page color "Sportraits" from *Sport* magazine; quickly delivering my copies of the Birmingham *News* so I could reach Rickwood Field early enough to see raccoon-eyed Eddie Lyons of the Barons arrive for another night's work. At some point in there I developed a fixation on Jacob Nelson ("Nellie") Fox, the runty, tobacco-chewing second baseman for the Chicago White Sox— I gamely tried to ape Nellie's huge chaw until the day I caught a bad hop in the throat and threw up on the spot—and when my parents casually mentioned that they had almost named me James Nelson Hemphill I sulked for three days. Nelson was my mother's maiden name; but hey, I could have been Nellie Hemphill.

By the time I was fifteen, I had determined that my fate was to play professional baseball. Nothing else mattered. One year I saw fifty of the Barons' seventy-seven homes games, usually sitting alone in the bleachers so I could dissect every move on the field, and coaxed my parents into making trips to Atlanta and Memphis and Chattanooga for Barons road games. "A man can do anything he makes up his mind to do," my old man once told me, avoiding the facts about my frail body. I merely got by in school, sketching uniforms and ballparks on sleepy spring afternoons when I should have been listening to science lectures. I had no hobbies and no interest in girls (except one, for a while, whom I ventured to kiss on the sixteenth date). Once I had delivered my newspapers after school on days when the Barons were on the road, I would bicycle home and continue preparing for my life's work: perfecting the hook slide on the rocky "sliding pit" I had scraped out beside the house, building up my forearms with a set of mail-order Charles Atlas hand grips, greasing the pocket of my baseball glove with neat's-foot oil, swinging my Jackie Robinson model Louisville Slugger in front of a full-length mirror, topping off the ritual by downing a pint of creamy half-and-half milk and a dozen fudge brownies and a raw-egg milk shake.

What was happening didn't occur to me at the time, of course, and would not occur to me until several years later. I had closed myself up in a fantasy world, a world where anything happens if you simply think it, just as easily as I nightly closed my bedroom door to go to sleep listening to Gabby Bell broadcasting the Barons games from Mobile. I put off asking swishy sophomores for a date until it was too late, because I was afraid they would say no. I did not go out for the high school baseball team—choosing, instead, to work and save my money so that I could attend summer baseball camps—because I was afraid I wouldn't make it. By avoiding all the commitments, I avoided the possibilities of failure. Perhaps no one realized this and suffered from it like my mother, who dreamed of my going to college and marrying a nice girl and getting a respectable job someday. "Don't you think you're missing out, son?" she said to me once. "On what?" I said. "On *life*," she said. I had no earthly idea what she was talking about.

The time to expose myself, to put it on the line, came early in 1954 as mid-term graduation neared. During the fall I had clipped an ad from *The Sporting News* that told of the Jack Rossiter Baseball School in Cocoa, Florida. For sixteen years Rossiter, a part-time Washington Senators scout, had been running the school during January and February for hopeful unsigned players, who worked out under the supervision of former major leaguers and scouts. "Players showing promise," the ad concluded, "will be signed to professional contracts."

The last month of high school was spent in a fog—doubling up on the exercise, honing the bat with a soup bone, buying a new pair of spikes and breaking them in—and on the final day of classes a teacher invited all of the graduating seniors to stand and tell their plans for the future. "I want to spread the word of the Lord," said one girl. "Sleep for about three months," drawled a gangly basketball player. When it came my turn I nervously bolted to my feet, solemnly announced my intention to "play professional baseball," and upon falling back into my seat had the impression that my classmates were noticing me for the first time. I had finally committed myself.

A week after the graduation ceremony, I threw my gear into my old man's truck—he had a load going to Miami and would drop me off in Cocoa—and we left home. The occasion was every bit as momentous for him as it was for me. He had never been allowed to play baseball as a kid in rural Tennessee, his mother being afraid he would get hurt, so he had lavished his love for the game on me. He had absolutely no doubt that I would someday play in the major leagues. Not an articulate man, now he could understand the need to say something lasting and important to send me into manhood. As the tires whined toward the Atlantic coast, we talked about Cocoa and baseball and the minor leagues. And we must have been skirting Jacksonville in the middle of the night when he went quiet for a while and finally, with a great clearing of his throat and much shifting around in his seat, blurted out the best piece of advice he could think of at the moment. "Always use a rubber, boy," he said.

I was deposited before 8 A.M. in front of the shabby tin-roofed Seminole Hotel, where all players had been told to report. Lugging a new cardboard suitcase in one hand and my bat and glove in the other, I checked into a room with oily wooden floors and a creaking overhead fan. Then I nervously walked the streets for an hour before I returned to the hotel, went to the end of the hall on the first floor and knocked lightly on the door. "It's open," a voice rasped, and I stepped inside. Jack Rossiter—a fat, garrulous man with bronze skin and blond wavy hair remindful of Liberace—was sitting at a desk in his shorts and undershirt, looking every bit like Sidney Greenstreet in one of those Oriental movies, sipping something from a hotel-room tumbler.

"Checked in yet?" he said after introductions.

"Yeah." *Be cool.* "I got something down the hall."

"That's strange."

"What? Sir?"

"You don't look like the type."

"Hunh?"

"Blonde, brunette, or redhead?"

"A room," I said. "I've got a *room* down the hall." Jack Rossiter, the major-league scout, was laughing uncontrollably now, his raucous strip-joint howl pounding away at me while I wondered what to do with my hands.

If Roger Kahn's postwar Brooklyn Dodgers were the Boys of Summer, then we were the Boys of Spring: the culls, the dreamers, the ones who now had to pay somebody to look us over. One was already twenty-five years old, just out of the service, figuring he might as well give it a shot before going to work for the rest of his life. Another was a deaf left-handed pitcher from North Carolina whose hometown had paid his tuition and given him a magnificent banquet before putting him on the train. A half-dozen had real ability and were quickly signed by Rossiter for the Senators' farm system, but the rest of us had little more than desire. As the weeks passed at the local ballpark, working out and playing games under an ex-shortstop named Eddie Miller and an old pitcher named Pete Appleton, a frantic dread set in with those of us who remained unsigned. Where do you go from the Jack Rossiter Baseball School? We might make the rounds of the Class D leagues, or we might stay another month in Cocoa, or we might say to hell with it. With less than a week remaining, we got a chance of sorts. A scout representing the Panama City Flyers of the Class D Alabama-Florida League came through with a stack of standard player contracts offering $150 a month if you made the club, lined up about a dozen of us who appeared ambulatory and broke out a pen. It must have looked like a straw boss signing up grape-pickers and onion-toppers off the back of a flatbed truck. That night, unable to sleep, I wrote cards and letters to a dozen friends and relatives to advise them that I could probably arrange tickets for the Flyers' opening game of the season.

Nothing went right at Panama City. Anxious to get away on the big adventure, I bummed a ride from Cocoa with a rangy lead-footed outfielder named Ron Horsefield and we left late one night, having convinced ourselves that we would be getting a head start on the others and that the long ride across Florida would be cooler then. We ran out of gas in one town, got stopped for speeding in another, and when we arrived at the Dixie-Sherman Hotel we discovered that we were a day late for spring training. It turned out the scout had signed at least forty boys like us, put them up barracks-style on the rooftop terrace of the hotel, and when Horsefield and I walked in they were walking out for the morning workout. In a panic, we eschewed sleep and rushed out to the ballpark. Not only had we missed a night's rest and breakfast, we found when we got there that all of the decent uniforms had been taken. Dressed like a circus clown, tired and bleary-eyed and thoroughly disoriented, I found that my legs wouldn't take me to ground balls and my arms could hardly swing a bat. "Jesus, kid," yowled a hairy veteran named Bob Karasek when I nubbed a blooper to right field, "you'll hit .300 in this league if your thumbs hold out." On the morning of the third day, with an exhibition game scheduled that night for Tallahassee against a Class B club, we gathered around the pitcher's mound. "Those whose names I call will be making the trip," said the manager, a career minor-leaguer named Roy Sinquefield. "The others can go." My name wasn't called.

It had not gone at all like I had hoped, of course, but I easily rationalized what had happened. Panama City hadn't been a fair test. I still felt I could play. Reluctant to go back home after all the boasting to my friends and relatives, I spent the next week at the home of my favorite aunt and uncle, in Dothan, a shaded town in the southeast corner of Alabama, which had a club in the same Alabama-Florida League. It was a listless week of sleeping late, watching soap operas and counting the stars. No one said much about what had transpired, knowing I must be working things out in my mind. After about a week there, my uncle made a call to a friend of his, the director of the Dothan Recreation Department, who arranged a tryout for me with the Graceville Oilers, just over the Florida line, about twenty miles away. I hitched a ride into Graceville on a sultry morning in early April and started asking around for the man whose name I had been given: Holt ("Cat") Milner, manager of the Oilers.

Class D baseball is a faintly-remembered piece of Americana that will never come our way again. It was at once the beginning and the end in organized baseball's classification system, a grubby underworld where young players began to climb to the top and where old players completed their slide to the bottom. Class D meant dim yellow lights and skinned infields and rooming houses and wild young pitchers whose fastballs could kill. You rode from town to town on condemned bulb-nosed church buses, watched out for beer bottles flying from the rickety wooden bleachers, showered ankle-deep in cold water, wolfed down hamburgers in desolate all-night truck stops and—if you'd hit a home run the night before—got out on the streets early the next morning in hopes of a free meal from an appreciative fan. Class D was survival of the fittest, a mean place to grow up, and if it was anything it was democratic. There were more than a hundred Class D towns in the country then, and on any given day in any of those towns a bus would stop long enough to let out a young man carrying a battered suitcase and a baseball bat, a teenager looking for the manager, looking for a chance. "We got three teams," went the saying, "one coming, one going, and one playing." The nucleus of most clubs was formed by the playing manager and the two or three others officially listed as "veterans" or "limited-service" players—their bodies having all but quit them, they led their league in hitting or pitching or savvy—but the real tone of Class D was established by the kids, the "rookies." It was their enthusiasm and their hopelessly wild dreams and their pubescent recklessness that gave Class D a reason for being.

There were strong D leagues and there were weak ones, and the Alabama-Florida was one of the latter. In the history of the league, only two players had ever graduated to the majors for any appreciable time, pitchers Virgil Trucks and Steve Barber. In 1954 only two of the league's six teams had working agreements with major-league organizations, while the others were forced to scramble on their own for uniforms and players and expenses. Dothan and Panama City each had a population of around 35,000, the rest being obscure little towns lost in the barren stretches where Alabama and Florida run together. There was Andalusia in Alabama, and Fort Walton Beach and Crestview in Florida along with the baby of them all, the town that would lead the league in attendance in '54, small but spunky Graceville.

When I tracked down Cat Milner, a droll fellow who was the only non-playing manager in the league that year, I discovered why I had been welcomed to try out. Only nine days away from the Oilers' opening game of the season, there was not a second baseman among the fourteen players in camp. "How come you got that hole cut in the pocket of your glove?" he asked me. When I explained that Eddie Miller had recommended it "so you can feel the ball," Milner shrugged like a man who had heard it all. Depositing my suitcase at a rooming house where some of the players were being put up, I walked on down to the ballpark and was told to pick out, from the clothesline strung to the low-slung concrete clubhouse down the right-field line, a uniform that would fit me. They were old gray road uniforms with patched knees and frayed sleeves and, across the shirtfronts, the dim outline of stitches left years earlier when the felt letters spelling CINCINNATI had been ripped out. I wondered, as I slipped into the shirt with the number 10 on the back, what Cincinnati Red had buttoned up the same uniform. I shook hands with two or three of the other players as they drifted in, finished dressing, poked a chew of Beechnut into my jaw, whapped my fist into the pocket of my glove, felt the smooth hickory of my Jackie Robinson bat, stomped my spikes on the rough concrete clubhouse floor, tugged at the bill of my Chicago White Sox cap, and burst out into the sun of the Florida Panhandle to begin my real life.

In retrospect, those were the most gloriously giddy days I have ever known. Most of the others were first-year players like me, and when we weren't going through the two-a-day workouts at the park we were hanging around the Circle Grille or riding to nowhere in somebody's convertible or merely sitting on cots in our rooms talking baseball. "Hey, roomie," a catcher named Tommy Doherty would whisper through his mask while I lunged away during batting practice, "better drop that stick and get your glove. You don't want to overexpose yourself." With Joaquin Toyo, the tiny brown Mexican shortstop, I worked out a sort of pidgin-speak so we could converse. "Dammit, this game's simple, boys," Cat would say during a break. "All you gotta do is hit the ball and run like hell." I couldn't hit a basketball with a paddle, but I could field. On my second day Cat came around taking orders for bats so he could notify the people in Louisville. That night there was a supper for the ball club at a local church, during which I was introduced as the Oilers' second baseman. In one week, on the night of April 15 at Wiregrass Stadium in Dothan, the season would officially open and I would become a professional. Again the cards and letters went out to Birmingham.

On the third night we had an exhibition game at home against a team from Fort Benning, Georgia, stacked with players who had been pulled out of the minors to do their military time. "Jesus H. Christ," one of them barked when they arrived at our little park. "I forgot Class D. They fed you guys this week?" I didn't know where I was most of the night. By the time infield practice was starting the little ballpark was crammed with more than a thousand fans, one of them my uncle from Dothan. The moment of truth had come for me at last, and when the crowd roared as we bounded onto the field to start the game I felt an elation I had never known.

We got pounded, and I struck out all four times I came to bat against Fort Benning's frightening left-handed pitcher, who struck out a total of sixteen that night. Cat was morose afterwards: "How do y'all think you're gonna hit old Onion Davis up at Dothan if you can't hit this damned *private?*" I had done well in the field, turning the pivot on two double plays and nearly throwing out a runner at third on a relay from the outfield, and I wasn't especially depressed when Tommy Doherty and I gobbled our hamburgers afterward at the Circle Grille. "Hey, that lefty got everybody" he said. "Anyway, if you don't play second base, who will?"

On the morning of my fifth day at Graceville, Tommy and I were the last to finish running in the outfield and break for lunch. The field was like an oven, our uniforms like wet blankets. Cat Milner stood down the right-field line, handing each man trudging toward the clubhouse his $2.50 meal money for the day. Exhausted but happy, we strolled up to get our money.

"One of y'all got change for a five?" Cat said.

"Not me," said Doherty. I shook my head.

"Gotta bust this thing somewhere."

"Hey, Skip, me and roomie'll split it," Doherty said.

"Won't work."

"Naw, see, we'll just take the five and —"

Cat Milner said, "I gotta let the kid go."

The blood went out of my body. I didn't know what to say. I wanted to lash out at the old man, but when I looked back at him I saw that after all those years it was still a messy business for him, having to swing the ax. I would never be able to hit Onion Davis, he said, and on top of that there was a second baseman coming in on a bus from Class C that afternoon.

The rest of the day was a mirage: jumping in the shower so nobody would see the tears, trying to tie my shoelaces with quivering hands, taking pats on the back and observations that I'd gotten screwed, never got a chance. Within an hour I had gone by the rooming house, had collected my things, and was standing beside the road leading back to Dothan and eventually home. It was only then that I let it fly, the huge tears streaking my bony cheeks and splaying my see-through nylon shirt. A farmer in a pickup stopped for me, surely noticed the tears, and didn't speak for several minutes. "Noticed your bat and glove," he said after a while. "You a ballplayer?" I said, "Sort of." They were the only words spoken until he stopped to let me out on the edge of Dothan. Still stricken with grief, unable to talk about it yet, I gathered my things, the glove and the bat and the suitcase, opened the door, and jumped to the ground. I looked up into the cab to thank him for the ride, but he cut me off. "Good luck, son," he said.

Life, 1972

4

Marty Malloy, 2b

THROUGHOUT THE FALL OF '93 and what passes for winter in his neck of the Florida outback, Marty Malloy began most days by driving his pickup truck to a construction site thirty miles away in Gainesville, the big city in those parts, where he stood around in the predawn hour sipping coffee from a paper cup and warming himself over a bonfire of lumber scraps, in the company of men with names like Cotton and Spiderman and Curly, while they all waited for sunrise and the foreman. For those other men, poorly educated laborers whose years were measured by a time clock, this was as good as life promised to get. They would needle him from time to time about his ballplaying, about how he would probably get so rich one day that he would up and buy his own construction business just so he could boss them around, but for the most part they spoke of joists and drywall and plumbing and women. He enjoyed the camaraderie and would laugh with them as they spun their tales of other jobs and other towns, and all in all he liked the work because it paid eight dollars an hour and it kept him in shape and it didn't take much thinking to pour concrete. It could be better—as it was for the players who had gotten signing bonuses so large that they didn't have to work at all in the off-season—and it could be worse. He shivered to think of working on the floor of a sporting goods store, as his best buddy in baseball had done one winter, because, to tell the truth, he didn't much like crowds unless they were in a grandstand, cheering, as he flew around the bases.

It hadn't been all work, of course. His main diversion had been the deer-hunting season. He and five of his childhood chums leased a hunting lodge, a ramshackle cabin in the hummocks of Dixie County where they kept their dogs in rickety pens ankle deep in shit, and with one more weekend remaining in the season he was sure to reach his limit of seven deer. There had been the football and basketball seasons at Trenton High, where his father was athletic director and head coach of the football and baseball teams; at the University of Florida in Gainesville, home of his beloved Gators; and on television, by way of a dish in the backyard that delivered the sports world to their den. There had been the trips over to the high school gym every other night after dinner, where his father served as a spotter while he spent an hour lifting weights to the twangs of Hank Williams, Jr.'s "A Country Boy Can Survive" coming from a boom box on the carpeted floor. And always there had been the more somber piece of new business that hung over him like a cloud: whether to marry the young woman who had presented him with a son during the summer.

Thoughts of baseball were never far away, just on the back burner. The mail brought *Baseball America* and *Baseball Weekly* and *The Sporting News,* a shiny new black Wilson glove from somebody in the Atlanta Braves' front office, a pair of batting gloves from the agent in Clearwater he had hired "just to get the other ones off my back," and a letter from the Braves telling him when to report to spring training. There had been phone calls from Tom Waldrop, the best buddy, who was, in this off-season, working as a personal trainer at a private health club in his snowed-in hometown of Decatur, Illinois; Waldrop delivered the news that their roommate from the summer before had been released in spite of a decent show of power and speed. Paul Runge, a manager in the Braves' farm system, who lived not thirty minutes away in Williston, Florida, also called, just checking in. In December, just before Christmas, Marty was a guest instructor at a kids' baseball clinic held by Santa Fe Community College, where he had been a star before turning pro. It had taken a full month to recover from the aches and pains of his first full

140-game season, but now some internal clock was telling him it was time to get ready to go again. Would he be returned to Macon? Promoted to Durham? Leap-frogged all the way to Class AA Greenville? Much would depend on how well he prepared himself in the next two months.

On a bleak Thursday toward the end of January, even as huge chunks of ice melted and fell from the cars and vans of snowbirds from Canada and the Midwest as they fled southward on I-75, Marty decided that enough was enough of this hibernation. He had barely touched a baseball since the '93 season ended on Labor Day, except for the clinic at Santa Fe, and the off-season, that dead time referred to as "the void" by baseball's poets, was driving him nuts. Stuffing himself with food, both at his mother's table and at a workingmen's buffet near the construction site, he had added nearly ten pounds and was close to the 170-pound mark suggested by the Braves. Sticking to his weight-lifting regimen during the winter, he had added muscle to his shoulders and thighs. He wanted to see how this new body felt, and a call the night before from the foreman on the construction job, saying the plumbers were dragging and he wouldn't be needed until the next week, had provided an opening.

Now, at two o'clock in the afternoon, wearing a pair of gray nylon wind pants and a thin T-shirt, he pounded his new glove, grabbed a couple of Louisville Sluggers, and trotted away from the brick gymnasium at Trenton High School. He tested his spikes in the end zone of the football field and continued onto the adjoining baseball diamond. Only yesterday, it seemed, this domain of the Trenton High Fighting Tigers—the gym, the stadium, the diamond—had been his world, the scene of many triumphs in all three sports. The same could be said for his father, Tommy ("Coach Malloy" in these parts), who now strolled in his son's wake. Wearing jeans and a sweatshirt and sneakers, he carried an aluminum fungo bat and boxes containing three dozen new baseballs still wrapped in tissue paper, as well as a stack of mail he had brought from the post office. Sullen gray clouds from the Gulf scudded across the menacing sky, threatening more cold wind and rain, maybe enough to kill the mosquito hatch in the swamps; but for now the temperature had risen into the upper forties and was sufficiently agreeable for their purposes on this day of a new beginning.

Marty was standing near the on-deck circle doing some light stretching when his father walked up and plopped the boxes of balls and the stack of mail on the soft damp ground. Wordlessly, they surveyed the familiar little ballpark, taking in the low rows of sagging bleachers behind the backstop, the telephone poles holding lights that looked forlorn this time of year, and the patchwork of dead brown Bermuda grass and bright green winter rye that swept toward the chain-link outfield fences. Marty pulled on his new batting gloves and took some swings to loosen up as his father knelt and began to unwrap the baseballs.

"Too bad the cage wore out," said Tommy Malloy. "You could take some swings."

"Nobody to shag 'em, anyway," Marty said.

"Maybe the Braves have got an old cage somewhere they could let me have."

"Not a chance. It's okay. I'll just bunt and take some ground balls."

"One of my kids ought to be here when school lets out. He can take throws. Hey, I almost forgot." Tommy rummaged through the stack of mail and produced a certified letter from Atlanta. "Your contract."

"Any surprises?"

"You aren't rich yet. They've got figures for Macon, figures for Durham, figures for Greenville."

"How much for Durham?"

"Eleven hundred a month."

"The extra hundred covers Corbyn [the infant son], anyway."

"It's just a start, son. That kid's expensive."

Father, son, bat, ball. Since the area around home plate was muddy, Marty took his stance on the lip of the infield grass. His father found a dry spot on the front slope of the mound, stretched his arms, gathered up a handful of the new baseballs, and began softly tossing them to his son. Marty bunted the pitches toward an imaginary spot down what passed for the third-base line. Not a word was spoken between the two of them, except for an approving "uh-huh" or "that'll work" from the father. The balls were turning green from the young rye grass, and when there was a cluster of them in a circle thirty feet away, the two would stop to collect them before beginning a new round. Soon the kid was dropping sacrifice bunts the other way, toward first base, and, finally, he began shooting bunts that were designed to skitter just past the pitcher for base hits.

All across America there were fathers who would kill for this: to have a son who played baseball, played it well enough to be regarded as a major-league prospect. The son was fortunate, too, to have a father who had played the game and knew very well the subtle joys that the boy was feeling: the smooth hardness and furled power of the bat, the ripple of the muscles, the approach of the ball; dump it, break away, hear them shout. They were in perfect synchronism, this graying father and his eager young son, embraced in a silent dance they had been performing for two-thirds of the boy's life. One could ask them independently about this and hear them stammer. "My dad played, you know; he's been there," the son would say. "Marty's had a thing for baseball from day one," was the father's feeble response. They were on the same page, more like best friends than father and son, and it was something to be savored rather than dissected and explained. Baseball and father and son were one and the same.

After nearly an hour of this, Marty tossed his bat aside, picked up his glove, and bounded out to the second-base position in his pigeon-toed trot. The school bell rang, announcing the end of classes for the day, and as the students spilled from the red brick building, one of them, a teenaged boy carrying a first baseman's mitt, peeled away and leapt over a low fence and trotted directly to the sodden bag at first base. From a gaggle of girls drifting along beyond the right-field fence came a shout—"It's Marty; hey, Marty!"—Marty responding with a halfhearted wave before returning to his business: smoothing the dirt with his spikes, jangling his arms and flexing his shoulders to get loose, spitting into the new glove and rubbing the pocket, then crouching to take the first ground ball of the new season. It came to him on three easy hops, slightly to his right, and he encircled the ball and gloved it and looped it to the kid at first base in one easy motion. *Thwack-scoop-toss.* Tommy, standing in the brown grass in front of home plate, took the one-hop relay from the kid, one of his American Legion team players, and sliced another one toward his son. *Thwack-scoop-toss.* Ah, to be twenty-one and undefeated. Marty moved with the ease of one who had merely taken a couple of days off, not nearly five months. Only when he flubbed a backhanded pick of a grounder far to his right did Tommy say anything—"Yeah, Tony Graffanino would like to see *that*," a dig referring to the second baseman immediately ahead of Marty on the Braves' minor-league depth chart—but for the most part it was the same wordless dance. Marty moved to the other side of the infield and took some ground balls at shortstop and third base, his throws getting stronger as he heated up, and after an hour of this they thanked the kid at first base, gathered the balls, and headed for home.

Home was a low-slung brick three-bedroom house set on a quiet corner of the little town of Trenton, nearly obscured behind palmetto bushes, oleanders, pines, and live oaks draped with cypress moss, less than a mile from both the school and the only traffic light in Gilchrist County. The Malloys had lived there for seven years now, ever since Tommy left the nearby town of Chiefland to take the job at Trenton High just as Marty reached high school, and by now it felt comfortable, cozy, lived in. Under a ceiling fan in the living room were a piano, a table holding a rotary phone, a formal sofa and matching chairs, and, flanking the mantel over a fireplace, framed studio portraits of Marty and his older sister, Amie. The carpeted den off the living room, dominated by a large-screen television set, a leather recliner, and a wide sofa, was the haven where the men could sprawl and watch their sports; on one wall stood a bookcase brimming with sports trophies and a set of faux-leather scrapbooks containing laminated clippings chronicling Marty's career.

His bedroom was down the hallway, next to his sister's and

across the hall from his parents', and the narrow single bed of his childhood belied the fact that this was the room of a young man who had already played two years of professional baseball and was now a reluctant father. A hat tree held the caps of the two teams he had represented so far, the Braves' farm clubs at Idaho Falls and Macon, but the room was still a teenager's retreat: a poster of Deion Sanders on the door, three new bats stacked in a corner, two walls holding photographs (Marty as an eight-year-old Little Leaguer) and plaques (one from the Future Farmers of America, presented when he was twelve, for successfully fattening for market a pig named Wilbur), autographed baseballs, pennants of the Florida Gators and the Atlanta Braves, a pile of old sports tabloids and magazines. Across the hall in the master bedroom was a stark reminder that life was shifting into another gear: at the foot of his parents' bed sat a baby's playpen, for their grandson's use during the long stretches when Marty was away playing ball.

Beverly Malloy was alone in the kitchen stripping kernels from ears of fresh corn when her son and husband drove up in their nearly identical Chevy pickups. She sat on a stool, wearing jeans, a handsome woman in her early fifties who ran the household and worked as an accountant for a veterinarian in Chiefland, ten miles away. Marty shuffled off to take a shower and Tommy retired to the den to read about the Florida basketball team's upset of top-ranked Kentucky the night before in Gainesville. Soon Amie got home from her job in Gainesville as a secretary in a dentist's office—reedy, twenty-four, with a squinty infectious grin, still wearing braces on her teeth from a near-fatal automobile accident a couple of years earlier—and as dark descended they all gathered at the dinner table to bow their heads and bless the bounty before plowing into Beverly's feast of fried chicken, creamed corn, mashed potatoes, sliced tomatoes, field peas, scratch biscuits, and iced tea.

At dinner, over the scraping of forks on plates, there was the muted chatter of small-town America: weather, neighbors, sports, idle comments on the small world around them. Amie pined for the day, not far away now, when her braces would come off. Beverly said the fresh vegetables kept coming in spite of the frosts, and it looked like the cold snap was about over; then added that Nikki, the young mother, had called to say she couldn't bring Corbyn tonight, but maybe this weekend. Tommy cleared his throat and said he had heard that Nikki had quit her job at the video store and was thinking about taking some classes at Santa Fe, and, "how 'bout those Gators whipping up on Kentucky?" "Wait 'til you taste my strawberry pie," said Beverly. Marty flexed his shoulders and said he had used muscles today that he'd forgotten about.

"You check on the dogs this morning?" Tommy asked his son while Amie cleared the dishes and Beverly dished out the strawberry pie.

"Left 'em a whole bag of chow to fight over."

"The one with the heartworm gonna make it?"

"I don't know. Hard to tell."

Beverly had been waiting to cut in. This was men's stuff, and she still didn't understand. She went ahead anyway. "Marty, why don't you just sell the things before you go?"

"They didn't cost me anything. They're for stud. Somebody gives 'em to you and you promise pups later."

"You can't feed 'em when you're gone."

"Scott and them will take care of 'em."

"But it's just something else to worry about."

"No problem. They'll be here when I get back." He grinned at his mother, hoping to close the matter. "A man's got to have his dogs."

By nine o'clock, Trenton lay in pitch-black darkness. The only places still open were a convenience store and the Gilchrist County Sheriff's Department out on the beeline road to Chiefland, a whitewashed cinder-block building where a dozen cars and pickups crouched in the brightly lighted gravel lot. Amie had gone to her room and was on the phone with a friend. The dishwasher was humming now as Beverly finished tidying up the kitchen. Tommy had rocked back in his recliner in the den and was watching a Georgetown basketball game on ESPN. Nearby, curled up like a baby on the sofa, his son slept and no doubt dreamed of spring camp at West Palm Beach. Fifty more days and nights of this and he would be on his way.

From *The Heart of the Game*, 1996

5

The Kid and the Third Baseman

Of all the stories about the special relationship that existed between minor-league baseball teams like the Atlanta Crackers and their fans, none is so poignant as the one involving a wide-eyed kid named Gene Asher and a veteran third baseman named Charlie Glock. The time was 1941, with the world perched on the brink of war, and the story of the boy and the man should shame those modern ballplayers who insist that $1.2 million a year isn't enough to play a game, who charge for autographs when they deign to give them at all, who have built an impenetrable wall between themselves and the kids who idolize them, who have left indelible scars on an entire generation of boys who might have become baseball fans.

Gene Asher was a child of Jewish parents who had suffered through the Depression, a thirteen-year-old who hawked peanuts and cigarettes and chewing gum in the aisles of Ponce de Leon Park—"Poncey," the Crackers' cozy home field near downtown Atlanta—because the family needed the money and he needed baseball. The Crackers that year were managed by Paul Richards, now in baseball's Hall of Fame, and the team was stocked with other future major leaguers like Connie Ryan and Willard Marshall. But young Gene quickly fixated on Glock, a twenty-six-year-old left-handed spray hitter who had failed to stick at the next higher level, with Indianapolis in Triple-A, but would find his niche with the Double-A Crackers of the Southern Association. At a salary of $400 a month, he would bat .311 with 120 runs-batted-in that year, and the team would win the pennant by fifteen-and-a-half games.

It was love at first sight. Gene was endearing, an earnest worker, obedient, a "good kid"; Charlie was regal, gentlemanly, straight-shooting, not rowdy like many players of his time. Married but childless, Glock seemed to look upon Gene Asher as the son he never had. Gene became known as "Charlie Boy" to the fans in the stands because every time Glock came to bat, the youngster would freeze, even in the midst of negotiating a sale, to yell out, "Come on, Charlie boy, you can do it!" The boy's adulation was such that he wrote a piece of doggerel and saw it published in an Atlanta paper: *No doubt you've heard of Charlie Glock / He hits the ball hard as a rock / He plays that hot sack very well / When he hits the ball they ring the bell . . .*

Indeed, the two became inseparable, like father and son, during that thrilling summer before the war would come along and change America forever. Charlie lived with his wife and their cocker spaniel at a residence hotel favored by many of the players, the 551 Ponce de Leon Hotel, a short walk across the street from the ballpark, and in due time Gene was dropping in to visit with them on the afternoon of games; then going into the Crackers' clubhouse while Charlie dressed, finally trotting onto the field to toss a ball and play a game of pepper with Charlie and the other Crackers. Such glorious days often ended late at night when they strolled off together, to the great envy of the other vendors and ball boys, for a snack or maybe even the twenty-five-cent fried chicken dinner at the White Dot Diner.

Then there was the night Charlie Glock came to dinner. Gene finally had screwed up the courage to ask Charlie, and was astonished when the invitation was graciously accepted. The date was set for the following Sunday, after a doubleheader, and when Gene rushed home to tell his parents the news rocked 501 Boulevard like an earthquake. Most of the fifty-odd Jewish immigrant tenants in the apartment building, including the Ashers, followed the Crackers either in person at Poncey or on the radio. *Charlie Glock? Here? For dinner?* Sure enough, on a splendid Sunday at dusk, having changed into clean sport shirts and gabardine slacks, the kid and the ballplayer strolled down Ponce de Leon Avenue side by side—Gene mimicking his idol's confident swagger, Charlie acknowledging the fans honking their horns at him—and when they arrived at the apartment building they heard a hubbub and saw the tenants leaning from the balconies or milling about in the courtyard, applauding the great Charlie Glock. Mrs. Asher had been cooking all day—leg of lamb, boiled potatoes, green beans, cornbread, apple pie—but she could have had canned tuna and spinach on the table as far as Gene was concerned. They talked baseball, *inside* baseball, until it was time for Charlie to go.

The tale didn't end there. Gene got fired the next day when he showed up at Poncey—one of his side jobs was to gather the rental cushions and put them away after each game, and the pal who had promised to cover for him had simply forgotten—but that was okay because he immediately got a job as a copy boy at the newspaper, his entry into a sportswriting career that lasted for many years. Charlie retired from baseball in the late forties, eventually moving with his wife to a suburban neighborhood, and took a job selling rugs at Rich's department store downtown. He and Gene talked periodically on the phone, and often Gene would drop by Rich's to stand at the entrance of the carpet department and solemnly call out through cupped hands, like a public-address announcer—"Now batting, number three, Glock, third base!"—which would bring Charlie shuffling across the floor for a laugh and a hug. It went like that throughout the 1950s, '60s, and into the '70s, even as Gene became a prosperous insurance salesman and Charlie began to suffer from heart disease and cancer.

Finally, on a day in 1980, Gene Asher got the word that Charlie Glock had died, at sixty-five, taking a large part of Gene's life with him. He drove to the funeral home and quietly took a pew, alone with his memories: of "Charlie Boy" and Poncey and the White Dot, of the night Charlie came to dinner. He expected the usual platitudes when the preacher rose to deliver a eulogy, but he was stunned, jolted from his reverie, when the preacher chose to do some moralizing. "Charlie Glock was much more than a baseball player," he began. "Let me tell you the story of Charlie and a little boy who needed a hero. . . ." Gene Asher, age fifty-two, broke down and cried like a baby.

Atlanta, 1995

PART TWO The Striving

6

Saturday Night at Dixie Speedway

ON THE LAST SATURDAY of June, while the Winston Cup boys were enjoying a rare off-week before plunging into a fierce stretch of fourteen races without a break, it would be business as usual for Rodney Dickson. All during the week he and the three men under his employ at Greater Design, a "landscaping maintenance" operation, had hauled their clattering equipment around the sprawling new subdivisions of Fayetteville, a fast-growing town some thirty miles south of downtown Atlanta, mowing lawns and trimming hedges and tidying flowerbeds in the stultifying Georgia heat, and now, finally, it was time to go racing. An energetic twenty-seven-year-old with bright brown eyes and a thick black beard on a chunky five-eleven, 200-pound frame, Rodney found himself suddenly leading the points standings in the Late Model division at Dixie Speedway, a classic three-eighths-mile dirt oval located in Woodstock, another middle-class exurban town thirty miles on the other side of the city, and if he were to win both the pole and the Late Model feature on this night at Dixie he would take home a total of $2,050 and move a step closer to the $5,000 bonus given to the track's overall points champion. Those figures paled in comparison with the phenomenal Winston Cup paydays, of course, but no matter. "Good thing I'm not in it for the money," he said. "Whatever I win goes back into the car, and it's a losing battle."

Rodney lived with his wife and nineteen-month-old daughter two doors down a country road from the roomy brick house where he grew up, and by noon he and his father, Jerry, a mechanic for the U.S. Post Office in downtown Atlanta, were hovering over the car in what amounted to their racing shop, a cluttered cinder-block garage under the trees in Jerry's backyard big enough to hold six cars, as they surveyed the damage. Rodney had won the Late Model feature at Dixie on the previous Saturday night but had wrecked the next night at the dirt track in Rome, Georgia, and he was worried that the chassis had been knocked out of alignment. Every night during the week, after finishing his day's work, he had gone over to the garage to work on the car with his father, who served as his mechanic and crew chief, and their assessment now was that it was about as ready as they could make it. Since they had no dynamometer, no wind tunnel, no track to test on, they were left to guesswork. If the alignment was terribly off, Rodney would simply have to drive accordingly.

Unlike the machines on the Winston Cup circuit, with their thin illusions of appearing to be production Fords or Chevys or Pontiacs, these dirt-track cars were pure lightweight racing machines of thin-rolled aluminum draped over an orange steel roll-bar cage. They weighed 2,130 pounds, against Winston Cup's 3,400, and their V-8 one-carburetor engines produced about 500 horsepower (against 700) to create speeds of up to 110 miles per hour on straightaways. Rodney figured he had about $28,000 invested in this one (and another $20,000 or so in the enclosed car-hauler parked beside the garage in the ninety-degree heat), and that he had driven it in more than fifty races over the past two years at Dixie and Rome and the half-dozen other tracks within a three-hour drive of Atlanta that he frequented. It was painted in a bright yellow with a white bottom this year, adorned with the number 18 and logos for his various local sponsors (plus the legend, "Thanks to Sonia Kayla," a bow to his long-suffering wife and daughter, who see little of him during the six-month racing season); outfitted with the same wide slick racing tires and rear spoiler and bucket seat and removable steering wheel of the Winston cars, but not much else. For starters, there was no windshield; rather, an angled sheet of aluminum soldered above the dashboard to deflect the mud and dust and bugs encountered on hot Southern nights at a dirt track ("The first thing you do when you get home is hose yourself down").

This was how the other half lived; automobile racing at the grass-roots level. Although Rodney Dickson of Fayetteville, Georgia, was faring better than most of his peers in terms of equipment and sponsorship and driving ability, he was representative of the thousands of young men who would be rolling away later in the day to the six hundred or more dirt tracks spread over the American landscape, primarily in the South and Midwest, to have at it on raucous little dirt "bullrings" carved out of the countryside. Soon there would be sightings on the highways of doughty race cars in tow, sporting hand-painted letters announcing their sponsor ("Joe's Garage") and some whimsical moniker like "The Other Woman," jouncing along behind pickup trucks crammed with the drivers' brothers and cousins and buddies who constituted their crew, all of them headed off into vigorous weekly combat in the mud and the blood and the beer. You could ask Rodney Dickson why he kept doing this week after week and year after year—spending all of that time and money, taking real chances on getting hurt when there was a family to support, having little hope that it would lead to much more than a scant mention in the Atlanta newspapers—and he would shrug and look you in the eye and say, quietly and firmly, "Because I love it." That seemed to be a sufficient explanation. About the danger of flying around those treacherous ill-lighted dirt tracks alongside wild-eyed rookies with more desire than good sense, he was stoical: "It's there, but except for getting my bell rung a couple of times I've never been hurt." That would change two weeks later at Dixie when he would go fender-to-fender with his father-in-law, Billy Clanton, and wind up with a badly wrenched wrist after a spinout.

His background was no different from that of most drivers who had gone on to Winston Cup: small-town, blue-collar, visceral, son of a man who worked on vehicles for his livelihood. Jerry, his father, "got interested in racing about the time Rodney was born, helping a friend who was into sprints, open-wheel, but I never had the money to go into racing 'em myself." Rodney began going along with his father to the races as a tyke, and by his early teens he was racing dune buggies and learning all about race cars by helping older friends who had managed to convert their street cars and run them on the local dirt-track circuit. The only other sport that had interested him was wrestling, but that ended with high school graduation. He scraped together enough money to refit his own car, a Vega, and when he entered it in the Cadet class for American compacts at Dixie Speedway, at the age of eighteen, he finished fourth. And he was hooked. They couldn't keep him away from Dixie, even when he married and began his own business and, much later, became a father. "He was a hard charger from day one," said Mike Swims, co-owner of Dixie Speedway. "There's a saying in racing, 'Go fast, go left, or go home,' and Rodney understood that right off. He's our Dale Earnhardt out here. I don't know if he gives any thought to going Winston Cup one day. His immediate goal in life is to outrun Stan Massey," a much older veteran in the dirt-track wars, owner of a wrecker service in the town of Mableton, the king of Dixie when he showed up.

At this do-it-yourself level, it paid to have well-connected friends. Rodney and his father did most of the work on the car during the week, and on weekends at the track they were joined by a reedy older man named Larry Watkins, who worked beside Jerry in the motor pool at the post office; Rodney's older brother Richard, a mechanic for Delta at the Atlanta airport; and any number of old high school pals who shared his love of racing. The sponsorship deals were laughable when compared to Winston Cup, but you took what you could get. Rodney's principal sponsor this year was Peacock Construction, a local firm, which loaned him a company truck to pull the car-hauler and bought him a new set of racing tires every two weeks or so (at $412 a set). Peacock's reward was to see its logo on the hood of the car, a facsimile of the multi-colored NBC peacock, and to hear relentless bleatings over track public-address systems about "Rodney Dickson in the Number 18 Peacock Construction car." Garner

Concrete Sawing & Coring was paying for all fuel; Active Auto Parts would sell him parts at wholesale, which Rodney said could mean a savings of nearly $3,000 a year; and the owner of RSD Enterprises, in the nearby burg of Rex, let Rodney use his racing shop whenever he had some serious work to be done. And that was it. Everything else came out of his track winnings and, sooner or later, his own pocket. "I had my best year in '95," he said with a rueful shake of the head. "Won fourteen thousand dollars. Went two thousand in the hole."

This was his tenth year of running a circuit of dirt tracks ringing Atlanta—at Dixie and Rome and Cordele and Hartwell in Georgia, Phenix City in Alabama, Greer in South Carolina, Cleveland in Tennessee—and sometimes it was possible to enter three races on a weekend. He had won "thirty-five or forty" in his time, almost always finishing in the top three or four, and he was happy to report that he ran "pretty good" at Senoia, a few miles south of Fayetteville, the only asphalt track he had experienced ("The difference is you can't slide on asphalt, and that's what dirt's all about"). Did that give him ideas about pursuing a Winston Cup career? "At my age I'm open to anything," he said. "Sure, I know the odds. You've got to move up one level at a time, first to asphalt and then to ARCA and then to Grand National. And, hey, there's only one rookie out of forty-something drivers in Winston Cup this year, right? Nah, I'm happy where I am right now. Mike [Swims] is right about me and Stan Massey. When he shows up, he's the man to beat. But I figure he puts his britches on one leg at a time."

The two rusty old water trucks had been at it since the sun broke over Dixie Speedway that morning: trundling down to the banks of the twenty-five-acre lake beyond a stand of trees encircling the property, siphoning water until their cylinders were full, bumping back up to the parched track, emptying their loads, going back for more. They dumped one hundred thousand gallons on the track every race day, and when it had become as slick as moss the water trucks were joined by a bulky ten-wheeled dump truck and even the early-arriving drivers in their race cars, all of them slipping and sliding until the mud had been packed into a glistening clay. "We tore up the asphalt and went back to dirt in '77," said Mickey Swims, a drag racer in his time who now owned Dixie and its sister track in Rome, about thirty miles northwest near the Alabama line. "We found that everybody likes dirt better. It might be ten times the trouble for us, but asphalt is three times as expensive for the driver because of tire and engine wear. The fans love dirt, watching those roostertails fly when the cars start sliding into the corners." He solemnly reported that there had been only one racing death in Dixie's twenty-eight years, that coming in the early 1980s when a rookie named Sammy Burks slid off of the top and had his neck broken when he slammed down against the pit wall.

There were three dozen race dates every year at Dixie (plus eight more at Rome, on Sunday nights), the total purses now having exceeded $1 million in one season for the first time, and before the schedule played out there would be some sort of racing for everybody. If it's got wheels, a Southerner will get around to racing it: Late Models, Super Late Models, Monster Trucks, Outlaw Pony Stocks, Modifieds, Sportsmen, Demolition Derby, Daredevil Motorcycle Jumps. (Once, at Atlanta Motor Speedway before a Winston Cup race, the drivers' sons furiously pedaled away in the Big Wheels 590, that being the length of the course in feet and the number on the dial of the sponsoring country music station.) The biggest event of every year at Dixie was the Hav-A-Tampa Shootout on the last weekend of September, the culmination of a series characterized by Mike Swims as "sort of the Winston Cup of dirt-track racing," with a prize of $30,000 for the winner of that championship finale. For three years running, in the mid-1980s, when Winston Cup drivers still could afford to mess around like that, the Swimses paid Bill Elliott and Dale Earnhardt $10,000 each to show up and race at Dixie ("Ten thousand fans, ten bucks a head, *sure* we could afford it," said Mike). There was seating for eight thousand—only a few hundred of those for the drinkers, exiled to undesirable rickety wooden bleachers on the turns—and the average attendance held at four thousand with hardly any promotion outside of word-of-mouth and posters nailed to telephone poles. Not until Tuesday did the Atlanta papers get around to publishing the weekend's local racing results, in a roundup on the back sports pages at that.

"It's a family operation all the way around," Mike was saying. It was five o'clock and the gates had just opened for the first fans to trudge in, some lugging seat cushions and coolers and sacks from KFC or McDonald's, most swapping first-name greetings with Swims. "There's Mickey and me. My mother runs the concessions and keeps the books, my sister handles T-shirts and souvenirs, and my wife does the computer stuff and stats. The drivers and the fans are family, too, sort of, since they come from around Woodstock and know each other in that small-town way." Soon he would be heading across the track to begin checking in the 150-odd drivers of every stripe who would be paying fifteen dollars apiece for an infield pass that would serve as their entry fee. "My dad warned me to do anything except go into race promotions, so of course that's what I chose to do. I tell you, I've never seen the same race twice out here, and when they drop the green flag the hair on my neck stands up and tingles. Bill Elliott and Jody Ridley are the only two we've had who started here and went on to Winston Cup. We've got an attorney, one of those kinds you see advertising his business on television, who comes here and races sometimes in Pony Stocks, in a four-cylinder Pinto. But the ones you've really got to admire are the guys who go to a job all day and work on their car every night and then come out here and drive their guts out on Saturday night so they can win maybe sixty dollars. They'll be here pretty soon. They're what Dixie is all about."

Just as there were people who had walked away from country music the day it went corporate and moved out of old Ryman Auditorium in downtown Nashville, and those who had turned to minor-league baseball in disgust after the unseemly major-league money squabbles that had brought on work stoppages in the mid-1990s, there were many longtime auto racing fans who would take a night at a Dixie Speedway anytime over the gaudy, expensive, and time-consuming spectacle of a Winston Cup race. Like minor-league baseball, stock-car racing at the grass roots was cheaper and closer and, in its own way, more plain *fun* for spectators. "I don't know if fans are down on Winston Cup now that it's gotten so big," Swims said. "I do hear some of 'em say they're getting put out about the inaccessibility of the drivers, the money they make, the ticket prices, the traffic jams, and all of that. It's gotten so big it might scare some of 'em off. A lot of our folks say they'll never go back to AMS [Atlanta Motor Speedway] until they do something about the traffic. But, you know, the television has gotten so good for Winston Cup these days, with the cameras inside the cars and all, they can come here on Saturday night without any hassle, bring the whole family and enjoy our show without spending a lot of money, and sit back and watch the big boys on Sunday on television. There's room for both of us, Dixie and Winston Cup."

The sun was hovering like an orange ball over the speedway as the three heavy trucks began circling the track, gradually tamping the slick surface into clay. There would be the usual full schedule on this night—three heats of "Bomber" divisions (a euphemism for street stocks driven by enthusiastic good old boys), a Sportsman race, Rodney Dickson's Late Model feature, a series of mad one-lap sprints by fans in the very cars they had driven to the track, all of it capped by a maniacal Demolition Derby—and the concrete grandstand was filling up in a hurry. Dixie Speedway sat in a natural bowl, less than a mile from an interstate highway spur connecting Atlanta to the north Georgia mountains, surrounded by rolling pastures that served as a parking lot, and was illuminated by lights on telephone poles ringing the grandstand and on two glistening new steel spires whose powerful beams were aimed at the backstretch. There was a twenty-foot-high catch fence around the outside edge of the track itself on the grandstand side, a gravel infield with cinder-block buildings holding concessions stands and restrooms, and an array of two dozen billboards on the backstretch advertising such local services as banks, wreckers, gas stations, tire outlets, and a radio station. While the public-address system piped country music, barely audible over the rumbling of the trucks, a woman sat calmly in the grandstand and nursed her baby.

By now, Mike Swims had set up for business in a one-room shack beyond the backstretch so he could record the entries in the Bomber division races. Thirty-two years old, with a full head of thick black hair, he sat on a swivel chair beneath a whirring window air-conditioner, wearing a polo shirt and blue jeans and sneakers and wraparound sunglasses. The Sportsman and Late Model starting positions would be determined in qualifying heats, but the entrants in Bomber and Super Trucks and Demolition Derby would have to draw for positions. The Bombers were the kids, the rookies, the guys next door who simply had a hankering to race—"what Dixie is all about"—and the three divisions were determined by their experience. They would park their battered heaps outside in the dust and step into the shock of the air conditioning, outfitted in the cutoffs and T-shirts and gimme caps and sneakers that were their racing uniforms, to sign in and draw a numbered chip from a red plastic dispenser shaken by Swims. There would be about sixty of them, and Mike knew the names and hometowns and car makes of nearly every one of them as he scribbled the information on sheets held by a clipboard: "Jake, how's it going over at Chatsworth? . . . Still driving that ol' Number 8 Pontiac, Bobby? . . . You mean four guys, four cars, four divisions? . . . Your daddy get over that heart attack? . . ."

He paused when one of them, a scrawny older fellow, said he would be entering the Bomber Two class tonight. "Wait a minute, you've won four in a row in Bomber Two if I'm right," said Swims. "Naw, five," he was told. "You win tonight, you're gonna have to move up a class, ol' buddy," and with that the fellow swelled up and grinned as though he had been promoted from Grand National to Winston Cup.

"Lookie here, Mike, I got a little situation," said another, a pear-shaped kid in a T-shirt and unlaced high-top basketball sneakers.

"Let's hear it," Swims said.

"It ain't me, understand, it's my sponsor."

"I'm listening."

"See, when we get out there and run around the track, helping y'all pack it down, mud gets all over the car and you can't read my sponsor's name no more."

"You could hose it down before the race."

"Naw, there just ain't enough time. I was wondering if maybe I could just bring an old junker over here for that part and then park it somewhere during the week. Run my regular car in the race. I'd leave you the key so you could move it if you had to, ain't no skin off my nose."

Swims said, "It's a good idea, but if everybody else did it I'd have a hundred cars out here all week."

"Like I said, I got to keep my sponsor happy."

"Tell you what, I'll bring it up with Mickey and let you know next week."

Rodney and his father had spent the afternoon putting the final touches on the race car—tightening bolts and belts, mounting new tires, filling it with gas and oil and water, hosing off the layer of caked mud from the previous weekend—and they were muscling it up the ramp into the car-hauler by the time the rest of the crew arrived. Larry Watkins and Richard Dickson would be joined this night by a teenager with his arm in a cast, Barry Peacock, son of the sponsor, and an old high school friend of Rodney's named Chris Peacock (no relation to Barry). They secured the car in the hauler with a winch, tossed in an extra set of tires and a floor fan and a cooler full of soft drinks and snacks, and then bumped out of the backyard and onto the pavement for the sixty-mile drive along Atlanta's interstates to Dixie Speedway. Rodney's wife and daughter and mother would follow shortly, when his mother got off work at the dry cleaner's.

By the time they arrived in the infield, at six o'clock, the place had the feel of a noisy convention—which it was, in a way. A dozen of the Bombers were still out on the track, groaning around behind the big trucks in low gear, helping to pack the surface into hard clay, while the infield rumbled and belched and farted with the thunderous cacophony of more than a hundred machines of every color, size, condition, and ilk: shiny new Super Trucks, long-snouted twenty-year-old Pontiacs and Oldsmobiles not seen much on the roads anymore, feisty little Pintos and Camaros wearing their dents and bruises proudly, crumpled Demolition Derby junkers marked for death. The lights came on, causing the cars to gleam under the pale glare, revealing their numbers and sponsors and mottos—"With God Your [sic] Always a Winner" and "Bearly Legal" and "Need for Speed"—while around each there whirled a ragtag bunch of grease-stained boys and men, family and friends, in earnest last-minute preparations. "Reckon them *tahrs*'ll make it? . . . Where's that five-eighths wrench at? . . . That sumbitch cuts in on me again, he'll hear from me . . . Earl, the motherfucker's gon' be too loose, I tell you . . ." In the middle of it all was a supply truck, a virtual rolling auto supply store, whose back doors had been swung open to display a cornucopia of emergency supplies ranging from fan belts and batteries to rolls of Bounty paper towels and spray bottles of Windex. There would be no ominous inspection station crawling with grim uniformed NASCAR technical inspectors, not here at Dixie Speedway, just one man wandering from car to car to warn against outside mirrors or oversized engines or a piece of dangling metal that ought to be taped down for safety's sake.

"They don't watch 'em too close here," Jerry was saying, stroking a close-cropped white Hemingway beard. They had parked the rig against a fence near the pit road and unloaded the car, in line with a half-dozen of the other better-heeled outfits, while Rodney went to the truck to wriggle into his racing outfit. "A man's a damned fool to spend all that time and money, and then have the race taken away from him for cheating. Fellow there"—he nodded to the red Number 47 car in the gravel next to Rodney's—"he came here from a different track, and after he'd won a couple of races they told him he'd have to change all kinds of stuff. Height, skirts, mirror. He wasn't cheating, he just didn't know." Jerry fished a clean blue rag out of his hip pocket, thinking to touch up the Peacock logo on the hood, and scanned the infield to see which of his son's big rivals were there tonight. He saw the 81 car of Granger Howell, a handsome thirty-four-year-old who owned a muffler shop in nearby Cartersville, a consistent winner at Dixie for at least a decade. He saw Phil Coltrane, owner of a speed shop in Canton, Rodney's closest competitor in the points race at Dixie. And then he saw the main man, Stan Massey, and a glimmer of envy flashed in his eyes. "Look at that. We're strictly family, but Stan's got himself some experienced mechanics, a regular racing team. He's been racing almost as long as Rodney's been alive. Well. He's here, and so are we." When Rodney emerged in his driver's suit, a pair of worn black Simpson shoes and a loose-fitting nylon jumpsuit striped in black, white, and purple, Jerry nodded toward Stan Massey's group. Rodney smiled grimly and put on his game face.

There would be twenty-two entries in the Late Model feature, the headline event of the evening, already being touted on the PA system, and as soon as the trucks and junkers finished packing the clay Rodney and Coltrane and Howell and Massey and the others were allowed a few minutes of "hot laps," like Winston Cup's Happy Hour, to check out their machines. Rodney put on his full-face helmet and crawled into his car and rumbled out of the infield to take a half-dozen laps around the track, swerving from side to side in order to heat the tires and to test the chassis alignment, floorboarding it on the straightaways, pumping the brakes in the turns, running high and running low in search of his groove. When he rolled back into the infield and parked behind the hauler only five minutes later, he was slowly shaking his head. There was much work to be done between now and qualifying, scheduled for immediately after the first race of the night, and the way that one went it looked like they might have all night to fine-tune the car. It was the first Bomber race, a fifteen-lapper involving twenty of the rawest rookies and the least dependable junkers, and a scramble that might have taken five minutes raged on for more than half an hour. They would barely complete one lap before there would be a spinout, the caution flag would go out, a tow truck would drag away the wreckage; another green flag, another crash, another yellow, more carnage.

The crowd was on its feet, laughing and pointing and cheering the bravado, loving every minute of what felt more like the running of the bulls at Pamplona than an automobile race.

Larry and Jerry had spent their time during the Bomber duel tightening lug nuts, lowering the gear setting, revving the engine so as to check the cooling system and the RPMs, topping the fuel tank from a red plastic gas can they had brought along, doing whatever Rodney recommended ("If the driver doesn't know what's wrong, who does?" said Jerry). When the winner of that first race had limped around the track, pumping his fist out of the window on a joyous victory lap, and the last Bomber had been dragged to the infield, it was time for Late Model qualifying. Each driver would have one lap to build up speed and two laps to establish a time. The four men constituting Rodney's crew grabbed white plastic bucket chairs and scrambled up a ladder to the top of the trailer while Rodney took his place in line on pit road, staring directly at the legend on the trunk of the car ahead—JESUS: BELIEVE OR BURN—and checked out the radio headset connecting him with his father, who stood on the trailer to get a view of the track. "Let me know the times, okay, the *fast* times," said Rodney. "Gotcha," Jerry told him.

The Late Models roared away from the pit road, each in its turn, throwing up roostertails of clay chunks as they got up to speed, then thundering down the backstretch on their solo runs. First out had been Howell, a crowd favorite, who once had entertained thoughts of going NASCAR but now found himself in his mid-thirties with a wife and two kids. "What'd Granger do?" Rodney said over the headset to his father. "Sixteen-thirty-four on the first lap and . . . hold on, here he comes . . . sixteen-twenty-six on the second," Jerry reported. "Where's he running?" "Low to halfway up." And so it went. Phil Coltrane, of the dashing name, turned the track in a poor sixteen and seventy-two hundredths seconds, "running low and doesn't look good at all." Rodney seldom qualified well, probably because he thrived on car-to-car competition, and this night would be no exception. His car was loose, sliding all over the track, partly due to the damaged chassis suspension, and he qualified twelfth in the twenty-two-car field with a time of sixteen-forty-three, which translated to 82.174 miles per hour. Stan Massey? On the pole, in a breeze.

When he rolled back into the infield and parked the car, nobody was smiling. His mother and his wife and daughter had arrived at some point during the qualifying. Sonia, a pigtailed blonde wearing hiking boots and tight denim shorts and a T-shirt, sidled up to Rodney, shifted Kayla to the other hip, kissed her husband on the cheek, and innocently said, "What's wrong, honey?" Rodney blurted, "The sonofabitch won't run, that's what's wrong." When Sonia flinched and nodded toward Kayla, cute as a Kewpie doll, he stroked his little girl's blonde hair. "Sorry," he said. "I don't know. We'll work it out." As the races continued—more Bomber races, then Super Trucks, then Sportsmen—he spent the next couple of hours wandering about the infield: worrying, thinking, checking to see how the track surface was changing as the night droned on, now and then consulting with his father and Larry Watkins. In the end, all they did to the car was adjust the spoiler to gain some downforce. "The track's gotten drier and looser, and this ought to make it stick a little better," Rodney said.

Finally, at ten-forty-five, it was time for the thirty-lap Late Model feature race. There were no pit stops at Dixie, due to the brevity of the races, nor any ceremonial call of "Gentlemen, start your engines." Rather, once the twenty-two cars had lined up in the order of qualifying, there was a wave from a flagman standing at the pit-road entrance to the track on the first turn, indicating it was time to crank 'em up. There came the same deafening roar of a squadron of engines being revved simultaneously, not unlike that tingling instant one experiences at Daytona and Bristol and all of the other stops on the Winston Cup circuit, and, with the fans on their feet to celebrate the moment, the flagman began officiously waving the cars onto the track. Bucking and weaving, jockeying for position, champing at the bit, eager to get on with it, being admonished by the main flagman in a crow's nest at the start-finish line to form eleven orderly rows, two-by-two, the drivers shifted into high gear after the second warmup lap. When they came around again, flying out of the fourth turn at about seventy miles an hour, they spied the mad waving of the green flag and gunned it. *They're off!!!*

Racing on a small dirt oval was an entirely different matter from cruising the huge paved superspeedways like Talladega and Daytona. There was some drafting involved, when the cars went nose-to-tail at more than a hundred miles per hour on the straightaways, and over the course of a long season the spoils usually went to the more powerful engines. But here aerodynamics and raw horsepower often would take a back seat to the sheer *arrogance* of a driver, his compulsion to let the others know *Outta my way, asshole, here I come.* Dirt-track racing was a three-round flurry of punches, not a fifteen-round war of attrition, and it was up close and personal. This was where almost all of the Winston Cup drivers had begun, and over the course of the '96 season more than one of them, during post-race interviews in Victory Lane, would describe his winning move as "a little move I learned on dirt one night at Hickory when I was just startin' out." Jerry Dickson said, "Yeah, but it's still about like Winston Cup. It takes three things: the car, the setup, the driver. No, better make that four. Takes luck, too." It was a mad dash of only thirty laps, not quite fifteen miles, a race that would take less than ten minutes were there no caution flags, and it could be won or lost in the corners, depending on how well a driver controlled his slides in and out of the turns.

There would be cautions galore on this night, a total of four, each of them resulting when two cars tried to muscle into a turn where there was room for only one, and Rodney managed to stay free of the early wrecks. "Go, go . . . clear, clear," he heard on his radio from Chris Peacock, his spotter during the race, who was standing on the roof of the trailer. "How many behind me now?" Rodney radioed after a series of moves on the corners had enabled him to begin picking off other cars, one at a time. "Twelve," said Peacock. "*Twelve?* That all? Damn." Stan Massey had avoided all of the trouble on the track the simple way, by staying out front well ahead of the pack, and his lead was growing on every lap. "Git 'im, honey, git 'im," Sonia was shouting, jumping up and down on the roof of the hauler, still holding Kayla on her hip, causing the hauler to rock. Rodney was on the back straightaway now, diving low and trying to take Granger Howell on turn three. "Git 'im, honey, git 'im, honey, git 'im!!!." Jerry stepped in front of Sonia and took her by the shoulders, mouthing something to her, and it worked only for a moment. Howell spun out and had to be towed from the track, and when the green flag came out again Rodney came up on the tails of two cars, both carrying the number 66, threatening to run over their backs like a rude tailgater on the interstate. *Git 'im, honey, git 'im.*

He picked off one of the 66 cars, to move into sixth place, but time was running out. The other 66, either unmindful or caring less that he wasn't allowed to be outfitted with a rear-view mirror at Dixie, began driving with the mirror. In the best tradition of Dale Earnhardt and the other superstars who had been teethed on dirt tracks, aware that the 66 car was keeping his eyes on him and him alone, Rodney tried feinting right and feinting left, but to no avail. The fellow was blocking him out, quite adroitly, countering each move. Rodney tried frightening him, literally bumping him, hoping his adversary would lose his cool for the instant it would take to get inside for the fatal tap on his left rear flank that would spin him out of the way. If it had worked, with the four leaders spread out the way they were, he might have been able to make a sprint to the finish line with Stan Massey. But, alas, time ran out. Stan Massey had won again.

Only when it was over and they were loading the car into the hauler did they notice that it had all taken place under the eerie glow of a perfectly full moon, as orange as the afternoon's sun due to the cloud of dust lingering over the speedway. Out on the track, like teenage hotrodders going *mano a mano* on a country road—*Rebel without a Cause!*—fans who had simply come out of the stands and fired up their street cars were now fishtailing around the course, two at a time, in one-lap scrambles. From the gravel parking lot on the hill beyond the third turn, a line of crumpled junkers began lumbering down the hill to the track for the grand finale of the evening, the Demolition Derby. A thick coat of red dust blanketed everything.

"The guy pulled the same stuff on me last week," Rodney was saying as he trudged toward the cinderblock building doubling as a concessions stand and a pay window. "You think he doesn't know you can't drive here with a mirror? I'd go after him, but the problem is he's a good guy, a friend of mine." Ah, well. Another night, another race. On the July Fourth weekend, while the Winston Cuppers were running the traditional Firecracker 400 at Daytona, Rodney would be chasing Stan Massey again at Dixie Speedway in a pair of two-hundred-lappers on Friday and Saturday nights, the latter paying $7,000 to win, then going on to Rome Speedway on Sunday night for the Firecracker 50. He stood in line for his winnings, $250 in cash, while his father and his brother and his two friends tied things down and locked the doors on the hauler, and they rolled away from the track at midnight. They stopped at a Waffle House near the interstate for a greasy breakfast and much animated discussion about the race, swapping friendly insults with fans who recognized Rodney, and they got home around two o'clock in the morning.

From *Wheels*, 1996

The Great Wallenda

EARLY ON A CRISP MARCH morning inside the bleak granite armory at Rock Island, Illinois, hard by the Mississippi River, they were busily setting up for the opening night of the annual Quad Cities Sports, Boat, Camping, and Vacation Show. The cavernous hall was a jungle of new boats and campers being preened and drawn into place by proud exhibitors while workmen swept out the grandstand and dumped trout into an artificial pond and finished nailing up exhibition booths. Still, the entire scene was dominated by one thing: the wire. The show would run for five days and would draw thousands of outdoor enthusiasts, resulting in many sales for the exhibitors, and the main attraction—the "hook," as promoters are wont to say—would be the appearance of the famous Flying Wallendas high-wire troupe. Every night at nine o'clock, and at matinees on Saturday and Sunday, ageless Karl Wallenda and the other three—a dusky Chilean named Luis Murillo and Karl's grandchildren Tino and Delilah—would squeak their resined slippers across the fifty-foot cable some forty feet above the concrete floor without the insurance of a safety net. A couple of weeks earlier at a Shrine circus in Madison, Wisconsin, the act had attracted seven straight sellout crowds of nine thousand each in three days, so the Wallendas were expected to move a lot of merchandise for the four thousand dollars they were being paid.

The wire was already up when Karl Wallenda wandered into the buildings at mid-morning. A dapper, broad-chested man with his mouth stretched in a perpetual sardonic grin, he had already purchased an elegant white-on-white dress and ordered a bright red $110 blazer, which he would pick up later in the day. "Too bad I don't have it for the television interviews," he said, peering up at the half-inch cable and then mounting the steps to the stage, where Tino sat cross-legged on the floor, braiding a rope. Tino had begun putting up the wire the day before, upon arrival from a circus date in Lansing, Michigan. Assured that the wire was solid, that the guy wires were taut and the two platforms were steady, Wallenda left the stage and began loitering around the floor beneath the wire as nonchalantly as if he intended to be a spectator rather than the star that night. "I don't have to check out the wire," he said, "because I have complete faith in Tino. After all, he is going to have to walk on it, too." There is never anything to be afraid of, he said, if you know what you are doing.

It was all very casual until one of the workmen passed by and chirped, "Hey, Mr. Wallenda, you gonna do that dangerous one tonight?"

"They are *all* dangerous," Wallenda said.

"Naw, I mean the one that killed all them people."

"You talk about the Seven-Man Pyramid."

"Yeah. The one with all the people on top."

Wallenda stiffened as he always does when the subject of the Seven-Man Pyramid comes up. It had been his dream stunt and the one he had worked toward all his life—seven people in a precarious three-layer pyramid on the wire at one hundred feet, without a net—but in Detroit's Cobo Hall one of them wavered and they came crashing down. A nephew and a son-in-law died, an adopted son was paralyzed for life, and Karl himself suffered a broken pelvis and a double hernia. The memory is so painful that Karl doesn't like to be reminded of it. "No," he mumbled to the workman, "we don't do the pyramid anymore. There are only four of us remaining." He was glum and distant for the rest of the morning.

Karl Wallenda has lived with fear and tragedy for most of his sixty-eight years. Born into a circus family in Germany, he has been walking the high wire for fifty-two of those years. In that time he has done many spectacular things—the most noteworthy being an eleven-hundred-foot walk across a treacherous wind-swept eight-hundred-foot-deep gorge in the Appalachians of northeast Georgia—and consequently he has been celebrated as few performers have been in the history of the circus. Ask the man on the street to recite some famous circus names and he will likely be able to come up with only three: Clyde Beatty, the animal trainer; Emmett Kelly, the clown; and Karl Wallenda, the high-wire artist. For risking his life on the high wire in any number of improbable ways, Wallenda has received as much as ten thousand dollars a crack and virtually transcended the narrow world of the circus.

But he has had to pay his dues. The first tragedy occurred in 1936 when Karl's youngest brother bicycled across the wire at an amusement park in Sweden but was thrown to his death by the high winds. Then came the 1962 Detroit accident, the most celebrated of them all, and three years later a sister-in-law was killed during her own high-pole act in Omaha. And finally, last summer, in Wheeling, West Virginia, his daughter's husband touched an exposed electrical clamp and fell seventy feet to his death. Now the scars on the sprawling Wallenda family, most of them cloistered around the patriarch in Sarasota, are permanent. His wife, who quit the circus fifteen years ago, refuses to watch a performance. Hermann, the oldest brother, was never the same after Detroit and quit two years later. Jana, a niece terrified and almost killed at Detroit (Karl dangled from the wire by his legs and held her for nearly ten minutes until they could get a fireman's net under her), promptly quit and went back to Germany to work as an usherette in a theater. The son, Mario, paralyzed and bitter, inspects contact lenses in a Sarasota laboratory and sees his parents only two or three times a year. Now Karl performs with yet another generation of Wallendas, his two grandchildren, and the possibility that they, too, might be injured or killed weighs heavily on him these days. "Rather than worry about them," he says, "I would prefer to work by myself."

It is difficult for him to articulate the reasons why he continues. Five years ago he tried to retire, to turn the act over to the rest of the family, but he went stir-crazy and returned after four months. "I guess it is—what do you call it?—ego." He says he *has* to do it. "I need to be up there on the wire, entertaining the people and hearing them applaud." On fear and the dangers involved in the act, which has never been done with a net, he is stoical: "It is dangerous. I know that. But the percentages are not that bad. Only one time has death come to the Wallenda family on the high wire. That was Detroit. Wheeling was not a fall. It was a crazy electrical clamp. We have walked thousands of times with only one fatal accident." Does he, the Great Wallenda, become frightened before a performance? "Sometimes, yes, on the night before. Once I have taken the first step onto the wire I am thinking only of getting to the other side. I tell you one thing, and this is no publicity or anything," he says, his steel-blue eyes going cold and blank. "I have one belief, that there is a God in the world. I believe that God stands by you. So any time I go on the wire I'm not alone. Every night I go to bed and I thank the good Lord that I still have the energy and can still do things. Then, when I have walked the wire, I have two strong martinis and I forget it."

Those around Wallenda have their own theories about what makes him go. "He is a ham, like all of us," says his daughter, Carla, who continued to perform on the high pole even after her husband was electrocuted at Wheeling. Karl, says older brother Hermann, "is afraid of dying in bed. He will go until he can't walk. It is ego, no doubt about it." To Jack Leontini, a longtime confidante who lives in the cottage behind the Wallendas' house and manages Karl's affairs, Wallenda knows no fear. "With Karl it is dedication," he says. "He knows he can walk any wire, anywhere. So there is no need to be frightened. He knows that if he concentrates on the job at hand and walks across the wire, he will receive the accolades that he needs." But to Mario, the crippled son, the reasons his father walks the wire are less mystical. "He knows what could happen, but he doesn't let it bother him, because it is the only thing in life for him. What else could he do for a living?"

• • •

Fear is one of our most elusive emotions, one that is often buried in the subconscious, and it is arguable whether there has ever been a truly "fearless" human being in the history of the world. All of us have our private fears—of dogs, snakes, water, social incompetence, heights, suffocation—which force us to face up to some sort of trauma, large or small, nearly every day of our lives. The over-the-road trucker knows he can meet death at any curve on the open road. The young mother lives with the fear of finding her baby has suffocated while taking its nap. The honeymooners worry about their first sexual performance; the aging libertine his or her last. The ways of coping with our fears are myriad: some psych themselves out of it, whereas others study their anxieties and conclude there is no reason to be fearful. But cope we must, however mundane the fear may be, or forever be haunted by hidden devils.

Then there are those who consciously put themselves in high-risk situations, actually challenging fear and danger: the automobile racers, the stunt men, the sky divers and the test pilots, the hard-hats who walk precariously along high steel girders. "You could probably call it a 'counterphobic experience,'" says Roy Grinker, Sr., M.D., a psychiatrist at Chicago's Michael Reese Medical Center. "They take these risks to show others they aren't afraid." And there is another, more fascinating, angle. "This fighter pilot, General Robert Scott [a Second World War P-40 ace who wrote *God Is My Co-Pilot*], wrote about how after a while the fighter plane actually became an extension of the body." Indeed, when a group of Royal Air Force pilots were interviewed after flying the saucy little Spitfire for the first time, to a man they described it as a sensuous experience: exhilarating, terrifying, almost erotic. If the fear of danger wasn't there, Dr. Grinker concludes, they probably wouldn't have tried it.

The Wallendas are ambivalent about this. "Sometimes I get scared," says Tino, the twenty-two-year-old grandson, "especially in a new place. Say, if we've been working in front of five hundred people and then we do it for ten thousand, or we've been working at twenty feet and then we go to a new auditorium and start working at forty feet." Many apprentices have been taught by Karl to walk on a three-foot-high practice wire, he says, but then have gone up for their baptism at forty feet "and come right down and walked away." There was one, Karl remembers, who had been performing successfully for some time, but one night in Mexico City "something snapped" while he was halfway across the wire and they had to go out and rescue him. The man never walked the wire again.

Perhaps the most eloquent of the current Wallendas is twenty-year-old Delilah, a swivel-hipped brunette of remarkable poise and beauty who has "had the wire out there in front of me" ever since she was a toddler and who was spanked by her parents if, upon losing her balance on the low practice wire, she simply jumped to the ground instead of practicing to fall and grab the wire. "It's not fear of the wire," she says, "it's respect for it. A little tension—or fear, if you want to call it that—is good. One reason my grandfather never lets us use the net is because he says we would get careless if one was there and we knew if we fell we wouldn't get hurt. Sometimes I am more tense than at other times, like when we are in a new place or we are rusty, but it's always good to be a little tense, and if you know what you are doing, and pay attention, and respect the wire, and understand the danger, you will walk the wire." Will she continue to do it? "It is the only thing I know. I love the feeling of being up there where there is danger. I could never drive a station wagon to the PTA."

By noon, following a live television interview across the river in Davenport, Iowa, Karl Wallenda had forgotten the conversation with the workman about the tragic Seven-Man Pyramid in Detroit and was in a chipper mood as we went for lunch across the street from the armory in Rock Island. Carrying a brown envelope full of contracts to be signed for upcoming dates, he fidgeted on painful bone-chipped heels injured recently when he lost his grip on the rope from the platform and had to jump the last fifteen feet to take his bows. "See if you can get her phone number," he said with a wink, nudging me and motioning to a lush nude painting on the wall. The hostess, who wouldn't recognize him later, to her embarrassment, finally gave us a booth in a dark corner of the restaurant.

"I tell you the truth, the only time I was ever really frightened was at Tallulah Gorge, in Georgia," he said in his heavy German accent as the waitress brought him the first of two martinis. Tallulah Gorge is a deep perilous canyon in the southern Appalachians, and as a stunt to attract tourists to the area he was paid ten thousand dollars to walk across it on an eleven-hundred-foot cable some eight hundred feet above the rocky bottom. For three weeks, at a total cost of eighty thousand dollars, a crew of forty strung up the cable. A week before the event Karl and his wife, Helen, set up their house trailer at the site and Karl checked out things and gave out interviews to an international press corps. "One woman called Helen and said she had just talked to God and God had told her Karl Wallenda was going to die. But those hypocrites don't bother me," he said. "What worried me was when this pilot told me the downdrafts are so bad there that light planes are not permitted to fly near the canyon. I was thinking of that when I got on the wire the next day. The wind was very strong, and when I looked around I saw no helicopters. Now, I know how to fall off a wire and catch it. That is why I am never afraid. But I thought to myself, 'If I fall and catch the wire, who is going to come and get me?' So I watched the wire and I walked as fast as I could." He also did two headstands for the crowd of thirty-five thousand, rushed into the trailer, and downed the usual two martinis Helen had already mixed for him.

He is, as it turns out, totally pragmatic about the dangers involved. He never practices anymore, he says ("At my age, why bother?"), and he is more comfortable walking the wire than flying in an airplane. "If something happens to the plane and I am sitting in the back of it and it starts to go down," he said, "there is nothing I can do. I am like this about automobiles. I want to drive it, not somebody else. I want to have control over a situation. If I die, I want it to be my fault." He is more nervous, in fact, when Delilah is on the wire. "If I am up there doing the tricks, it is all right. But when I am on the platform watching her

I get pools of water in my hands. I tell her, 'Delilah, be careful, my granddaughter,' and most of the time she laughs at me. She is a cold one."

"Could you teach me to walk the wire?" I asked him.

"Sure. I taught Luis in six weeks."

"But I've got acrophobia. Fear of heights."

"Have you played sports?"

"Baseball. A long time ago."

"Well," he said, "it doesn't matter either way. What matters is whether you *want* to walk the wire. No. What matters is whether you *need* to walk the wire. You must be a little afraid, and you must want to prove you are not afraid. Then. Then you can walk the wire."

Almost from the day he was born out of a suitcase in 1905, Karl Wallenda has had a need to perform. His parents, like their parents before them, had a small traveling outdoor vaudeville show in which the entire family was expected to participate. When Karl was five he was being hurled through the air by his parents, who specialized in trapeze, and by the time he was seven he was doing handstands atop church steeples to draw attention to the show when it hit new towns. "I had to do a lot of clowning, too, and I never liked that, because a clown had to be a dumb guy, and I never liked being a dumb guy." Karl attended some 160 different schools during those years, some of them for only a week, and at one point (when his father ran out on his mother) did handstands in taverns to bring in money for the family. "Even when I was able to go to school I would sit in class and draw sketches of the circus. Always I was dreaming of the circus."

His introduction to the high wire came when he was fifteen and, faced with another off-season working in the Alsace-Lorraine coal mines, read an ad in a newspaper for "a man that could do handstands for an aerial act." He took the train to Breslau and met a man who had put up a sixty-foot-high wire and was trying to start a sensational new stunt: the man would do a headstand on the wire, a woman would hang below the wire by her teeth, and another man—young Karl Wallenda, if he made it—would do a handstand on the man's feet. "I found out that fifty had quit before I got there. I thought, 'This man is crazy. I'm a guinea pig.'" But he had no money to return home, so he lied about his age and worked on his handstands at night in a grim room and, three days later, won the job. "I just did it. It is that simple. I did it." It was the making of the Great Wallenda. A year later he was starting his own successful high-wire act at Berlin's Winter Garden, and in 1927, he accepted an offer to go to Cuba for a year. ("What could I do in the wintertime in Germany?")

It was in Cuba that the first Wallenda family troupe was formed, with Karl and his wife and brother Hermann and a man named Joe Geiger. They were discovered by John Ringling. In April of 1928 they opened the Ringling Brothers Circus at Madison Square Garden to a capacity house, the four of them forming a three-level pyramid with the use of balancing poles and a chair, getting a fifteen-minute ovation. More than seventeen years later Karl was playing with the notion of the Seven-Man Pyramid when John Ringling died, and Ringling's successor, John North, "thought the idea was crazy and wasn't interested," according to Wallenda. Just after the Second World War Wallenda quit Ringling Brothers to start a renegade circus that lost a hundred thousand dollars in one year (at a time when he was methodically paying to get thirty-seven relatives and friends out of postwar Germany). He then went on his own, with his family act, where he has been ever since.

Today the Wallendas live in quite another world from that inhabited by most of the circus people who cluster around the shabby "winter quarters" on the edge of Sarasota. Karl and Helen Wallenda live in a tidy two-story white frame house in a shaded neighborhood close to downtown and are constantly seen around Sarasota society. Karl is a four-time past president of Showfolks of Sarasota, the seven-hundred-member circus organization, and he averages one hundred pieces of mail each week. Every afternoon when he is at home, promptly at three-thirty, the spacious side yard fills up with cars as friends drop by for a ritualistic cocktail hour. An old-country burgher whose only hobbies are playing penny-ante poker with circus cronies and collecting spoons from around the world (he has a collection of 740 of them, valued at twelve thousand dollars, and has willed the collection to the Circus Museum in Sarasota), he is your basic patriarch ("Karl is sometimes too kind and considerate to others for his own good," says a friend, explaining why Wallenda is not a rich man by any means). The only discordant note in the life of the Great Wallenda, in fact, seems to be found in the curious situation surrounding Mario, the adopted son, who was paralyzed at Detroit. Mario seldom comes around anymore, although there is a specially constructed ramp beside the Wallenda house to accommodate his wheelchair. "I have to read the papers to keep up with him" says Mario, with some sarcasm. Mario is now thirty-two, with a family of his own. "I don't regret what happened. Sure, I wish I could walk. But I knew what could happen. If you play with fire, you're gonna get burned. Everybody knows that except Karl. The thing is this: he doesn't care."

By nine o'clock at night, shortly before they would take to the wire for the first time in Rock Island, a tinge of anxiety noticeably visited Karl Wallenda and his two grandchildren and Luis Murillo. Karl had spent the afternoon doing more interviews and taking a short, fitful nap in his motel room. Delilah had worked four hours on the floor of the auditorium as a "computerized fortune-teller" at $1.65 an hour ("I can eat on this and put the rest in the bank"). Tino and Luis had double-checked the guy wires, to make certain they were still taut, before sleeping through the afternoon themselves. Now, dressed in the flashy sequined costumes sewn by Helen Wallenda, they nervously prowled about the cramped, cold dressing room beneath the stands while a pair of young men warmed up the crowd by doing acrobatics on a trampoline set on the stage beneath the wire.

"How is the crowd?" Wallenda asked the promoter, an amiable crippled fellow from St. Paul who had booked the Wallendas before.

"Not a thousand yet."

"First night's always bad."

"Yeah, and it's Ash Wednesday."

"No kidding?"

"How was I supposed to know that?"

Wallenda took Delilah aside and told her about some changes. Tonight, for the first time, it would be she rather than Karl on the chair balanced on a rod held by Tino and Luis. "Just take it easy and don't be afraid," he told her. Staring aimlessly at the wall, she smiled faintly and said, mocking him, "Yes, Grandfather." Wallenda burst into a grin. "One time," he said to someone in the room. "If only one time she would admit to me that she is afraid."

And the show went on. Karl Wallenda walked across the wire, followed by the others, as the crowd hushed and the band played circus music. Then came Luis on a bicycle and Tino behind him and Karl with a headstand and Delilah with a handstand and Delilah on Tino's shoulders as he bicycled across. Gasps and applause came from the crowd, act after act, until finally the lights went down and the band built to the finale in this bleak little auditorium in the middle of America. Lights down, music up, for the Great Wallendas. Tino and Luis edged across the wire, a metal pole secured at each one's waist, with Delilah perched on a chair supported by the pole. Once they reached the center of the wire, they stopped. Karl stood on the platform, a microphone strung around his neck, and, with a bit of show biz, pretended to have sweaty palms as he implored them. "Careful Delilah, careful," he said. "Don't lean too far, darling. Not too far. Don't hurt yourself." They made it, to great applause.

Today's Health, 1973

8

The Boys of Stalag Thirteen

NOBODY COULD REMEMBER PRECISELY how or when it became stigmatized as Stalag Thirteen, but its residents had heard quite enough about how adversities can be turned into blessings. For one month the dozen men who lived in the basement of the brick building out there on West Washington Avenue, on the seedy working-class fringes of Charleston, West Virginia, had lived in squalor without visible means of support. Nobody had a job. The lucky ones had girlfriends in distant towns who sent meal money now and then. They had a tiny black-and-white television set and bare mattresses on the concrete floor and an odorous one-man toilet and a pay phone across the street in front of a cut-rate pharmacy and a lot of time on their hands. Now and then a gaggle of groupies would ride by in an old Chevy convertible and shout, "Y'all with the Rockets?" and the first ones up from their stupor would say, "Be there quick," throwing on their cleanest dirty clothes and vaulting into the back seat in hopes of the first decent meal since the wife of the owner of the Charleston Rockets came by with a pot roast and some potato salad on Mother's Day. "Friend of mine the other day," one of them was saying, "he say, 'You call this pro football? Baloney.' So I say, 'Baloney? You got it right. That's all I been eatin' for four weeks. *Baloney.*'" The others merely shrugged. By now they were too old to cry, but it hurt too much to laugh.

Endure, survive, prevail. Those were the operative words for the boys of Stalag Thirteen, and what brought them together in the spring and summer of 1982 was a very simple dream, shared by all: they would endure the inhumanities of Charleston's armpit and survive the nondescript trench warfare of a shabby summertime semiprofessional football league in order to ultimately prevail by being discovered and signed to a fat contract by one of the twenty-eight teams in the National Football League.

Ah, the NFL, Valhalla to the millions of America males of all ages whose autumn lives revolve around a game played with a ball pointed at both ends. In the middle of '82, before an ill-advised players' walkout and the formation of a rival league (the United States Football League) and an over-saturation of games on television, the NFL was still a fairyland for anyone who ever donned shoulder pads. It was a land where network television generated $332 million; where a running back named Walter Payton earned $500,000 in a season; where the average player salary hovered near $90,000; where a player whose team went on to win the Super Bowl would receive an additional check for $32,000; where a sixty-second commercial during the Super Bowl telecast cost $750,000; where a retired superstar like O. J. Simpson could name his price for dashing through an airport in behalf of Hertz Rent-a-Car. And a place where some 250 positions opened up each year.

None of this was lost on the thirty-seven men who had slipped into Charleston on the first day of May, 1982, in hopes of landing a spot with the Charleston Rockets of the American Football Association. And it seemed, upon closer inspection, that the whole lot had been ordered up from central casting. The owner was an amiable native hobbyist, David Ferrell, whose Tape City outlets were suffering as he juggled money and stroked mutinous players. His wife played den mother to the boys of Stalag Thirteen and the three others living in her basement. Their daughter was the leading lady of a leggy halftime troupe named the Rockettes. The coach was a bearish former NFL star, Lonnie Warwick, who ran a tavern down the road. The quarterback, one of the few of them lucky to have a job of any kind, was night security officer at the county dump. The return specialist was a local hero with world-class speed and world-class problems. Almost all of the players claimed previous tryouts with NFL teams (meaning that, in most cases, they had run some wind sprints or thrown a few passes under vague conditions). So you had this smorgasbord of thirty-seven souls, desperately struggling to find the end of a rainbow they knew was out there somewhere, plopped in the midst of 63,000 people up and down the Kanawha River who fully understood their situation because many of them, too, had been there.

It was with this in mind—the near-impossible dreams of thousands of former college players to make it to the NFL—that a former Texas Tech Red Raider and Philadelphia Eagle named Roger Gill had founded the AFA in 1977. Going into its sixth season, the league had expanded to eighteen teams in a dozen states. The season was to begin on May 29th and end with a championship game, the American Bowl, on August 21st. Nobody was on salary, and once they got to playing real games each player was to receive one percent of the gate, minus certain expenses, for each home game. "Showcase, that's the working word for us," said Gill from the league office in San Antonio. "There are thousands of excellent football players out there who feel they never got their chance with the NFL and in a lot of cases it's true. If the computers and the stopwatches say a kid isn't worth a shot, he doesn't get a shot. So we know we can find the players. But right now our main purpose [as a league] is survival. We need local owners. Everywhere we've had failures it was because of outside ownership. The operations that have been successful have been run by local people with a reputation at stake."

With that as a criterion, the Rockets' Dave Ferrell was perfect. Ferrell, forty-five, had spent his life in Charleston, as an athlete and a sports enthusiast and a businessman; he was known around the valley as a man who paid his bills. He first became involved with the Rockets when they were formed in 1980. He was a minority stockholder in the beginning, the sort of man who proudly bought blocks of season tickets and even helped videotape the games for the coaches "just for something to do," but when he took a closer look at the operation the next year he was appalled at what was happening to the money. The Rockets had won the AFA championship for the second straight year, drawing nearly seven thousand fans per game, but were $109,000 in debt. It was either fold the team or find a buyer who thought he could clean up the mess and keep them in love-starved Charleston. Ferrell bought the Rockets. "Why me?" he tried to explain one day in his musty office above Stalag Thirteen. "I guess I'm into it for the same reasons the players and the coaches and the fans are. I love football, and I'm a dreamer."

They were tired enough as it was when they drifted into the locker room beneath the stands at picturesque Laidley Field, a trim stadium of eighteen thousand seats and artificial grass that sits between the railroad tracks and the interstate near the state capitol, to begin the business of taping and dressing and psyching themselves up for the regular-season opener on the last Saturday in May. On the other side of the field would be the Virginia Chargers, whose bus from Alexandria, painted a hideous green, was already parked inside the stadium gates. The word on the Chargers was that they had been slapped together in only two weeks, hardly enough time for them to get acquainted, but the Rockets couldn't care less. Their anxiety level was so high after all of the frustrations of the month that they were prepared to bare-knuckle the Dallas Cowboys on the street.

Ferrell had every reason to expect a crowd of ten thousand for the game. But at four o'clock in the afternoon the radio and television stations had begun announcing tornado alerts. An hour of so before the kickoff the skies were black and swirling and the rain was slashing like a tiger, and there were exactly thirteen umbrellas popped open in the stands, like toadstools, when the lights came on. Ferrell and Lonnie Warwick stood in the end zone, wearing slickers and frowns. "We could play tomorrow afternoon, but then we'd have to pay to put Virginia up in a motel for the night," Ferrell was saying.

Warwick, who knows his football players, said, "Telling these guys they can't play tonight is like telling a guy at a strip joint he can't look at the broads. They're ready to kill somebody. We gotta let 'em loose." He walked in the Rockets' dressing quarters and gave them the word and they began stuffing each other into their pads and their new red-white-and-blue uniforms ("Hey, man, when they play that 'Star-Spangled Banner' they ain't gon' salute the flag, they gon' salute *us*") and listening to their boom boxes as they tied their shoelaces and slammed each other on the shoulder pads. "They talk about how us bloods can't swim," said a black player, "but I'll tell you something; I can swim all right but I ain't fast enough for that lightning. Keep 'em away from the goalposts." And, from another, "If them guys ain't out there at eight o'clock sharp, we'll go play 'em in the locker room."

"All right, guys, circle around," said Warwick. "The Rev wants to talk." The Rev was an Episcopal priest, a benign sort in his black suit and white collar, a man who takes his football and his God seriously. The players went to one knee in a reverent circle as he began to pray.

"Dear Heavenly Father . . . give us strength . . . thanks for giving us the opportunity to bring joy to our fellow man . . . and no serious injuries. Amen."

"A-*mennn!!*"

"All right, dammit!" Warwick shrieked, jolting the players back to the matter at hand. "Those wimps know who the champions are and they've come down here to kick butt! Go out there and show 'em something!" The players nearly flattened him as they exploded, screamed, and clattered down the tunnel leading to the monsoon on the field. Left in their wake, Warwick lowered his voice to the preacher—"Thanks, Rev"—and followed his charges.

It was a fiasco from beginning to end. Virginia had failed to furnish a numerical roster, and when one was hastily assembled it showed five duplicate jersey numbers. The rain never let up. The Virginia Chargers played as though they had been introduced on the bus. Rocket Mike Tyson, a blur of a scatback, dazzled by returning a kickoff 99 yards for a touchdown and scoring two more on scintillating punt returns of 79 and 64 yards. The Chargers were fumbling center snaps, running into each other, dropping passes, and glancing wistfully toward the bus for Alexandria. The final score was 71–7. The paid attendance was 532.

Afterwards, they gave the game ball to Mike Tyson and tossed their jockstraps and socks and uniforms into piles, showered and dressed and, for those who could afford a drink or two, moved en masse to a bar called The Roaring Twenties to drink and dance and try to forget. "If Lonnie called a workout for tomorrow," said Terry Rusin, the free safety, "he'd have to send ambulances." And they went home, wherever that might be.

The next afternoon found the boys of Stalag Thirteen battered and restless. The torrential rain of the night before, which hadn't stopped until well after midnight, had created a shimmering heat beneath the blazing sun hovering above West Washington Street. They weren't talking much about the debacle of the night before, and what conversation there was came in the form of muffled random remarks, with the resigned cynicism once heard at listless remote Green Beret outposts in Vietnam. The little television set was on, and they would watch Mean Joe Green swallow his Coke and toss his jersey to a boy in the commercial famous at the time ("Here, kid. . . ." "Gee, *thanks,* Mean Joe") and somebody would say, "Gee, thanks, Mean Joe, I could live a year on what that jersey's worth on the street." Some tried to sleep atop the sweat-sopped mattresses, some watched with indifference as Kareem Abdul-Jabbar flipped his sky-hook over the Philadelphia 76ers in an NBA playoff game, and others stood around outside watching a 230-pound tight end named Eric Hegrenes polish and tune his black Honda motorcycle prior to riding it back home to St. Paul in the cool of the night. Rick Nash, a wide receiver from Idaho State, would later walk across the street to the Rite Aid discount pharmacy and drop a dime into the pay phone on the sidewalk and say to David Ferrell at home, "Eric's gone," then return to the shade of a tree.

The next day was Memorial Day and it brought the usual glut of patriotic shenanigans to downtown Charleston—bands, floats, majorettes, American flags, VFW pins and caps, crippled veterans in wheelchairs, pickup trucks with AMERICA: LOVE IT OR LEAVE IT bumper stickers, political speeches and preachers raging against atheists and communists and anybody else deserving the eternal flames of hell—but out there in suburbia, in his comfortable split-level home, Ferrell was in no mood to celebrate. He was, in fact, mowing the lawn. His wife, Pauline, was doing some cooking. Their daughter, Robin, was moping around the house because the Rockettes had had to trash their dance routine because of the weather Saturday night. Ferrell stopped to fix a glass of iced tea and, wearing his Rockets cap and T-shirt, sat on the patio and assessed the damage. "Yeah," he said, "I've been looking at the figures. Awful. We lost close to eighteen thousand dollars. I never saw weather like that in my life. Couldn't believe it. I mean, if we'd had a crowd of six thousand it would have been fantastic. Now we've got our feet in a hole it's going to take all season to get out of." The phone rang. It was Rick Nash, he was told, calling again from the pay phone across the street from Stalag Thirteen. Ferrell came back to his lawn chair. "Nobody else has left yet."

"You think they will?"

"Who knows?"

Larry Delwiche, the punter and one of the fortunates living not at Stalag Thirteen but in the Ferrells' house, walked past. "When they see the paycheck," he said.

"If they leave, they leave," Ferrell said. "I can't say I blame 'em. But I'm absolutely not going to spend any more money. I can get out even-Stephen if I sell in the next thirty days. We could fold right now, I guess, but I'm not going to do that if I really believe in what brought me into this in the first place."

The money wasn't a major factor for at least one of the players. Although his goal was the same, to be invited to a big-league camp, the single anomaly in a motley collection of generally aimless souls was a free safety by the name of Terry Rusin. He was renting a small house and had a steady girlfriend and worked at not one job but four: leasing fleets of cars for Vince Paterno Pontiac, selling jobs for a local printing company, helping out at a friend's three franchised Nautilus Fitness Centers in the valley and, not the least, playing for the Rockets. While the others were working as security guards or lifting heavy stuff or pleading for part-time work or wasting away at Stalag Thirteen, Rusin was living on the better side of the tracks. He had one of Vince Paterno's demonstrator models at his disposal. He had the keys to all of the Nautilus gyms and could work out at three o'clock in the morning if he felt like it. He wore trim suits on the air-conditioned sales floor of Paterno's. He ate steaks and drank good whiskey when he and his girlfriend, a pert dance instructor named Debbie, went out at night. Terry Rusin, unlike most of the others, had his life under control.

"I guess I live my life like a free safety," he was saying on Tuesday, the day after Memorial Day, as he checked around his modest frame house near the stadium. "I could never work nine-to-five. I've got to use my wits and my instincts and be free to take advantage of situations." Two of the players had been living at his house but had found another place, so one of his projects for the week was to spring a couple from the Stalag. "I can't stand to see somebody having to live like that. I've moved around in my time, but I've always had an ace in the hole: someone to live with, a source of money, something. Like when I played with Birmingham, I lived with my sister." He didn't need a place to stay, anyway, he said, because he was too busy. Sometimes he just flaked out at one of the gyms.

A scholarship player at Wayne State University in Detroit, Rusin had led the NCAA's Division II in interceptions one year and the NFL scouts were interested. The Pittsburgh Steelers had scouts in the stands during the Mid-America Conference championship game when, on the third play of the game, he knocked out himself and the man he was covering. He awoke on the bench, glanced over his shoulder, and saw the scouts leaving. They never came back. Rusin spoke for all of the Rockets: "Anybody in this league will tell you he didn't get a fair shot. That's what the AFA is all about. It's the computers now. Lydell Mitchell ran a five-flat forty, and the computers said there was no way he could make it. What happens? He becomes one of the premier running backs in the NFL. The computers are playing with people's lives."

• • •

Later that afternoon the big moment arrived: payday. The players, assembled in the locker room in their helmets and shorts and cleats, knew the figures before anybody had to tell them. Lonnie Warwick praised Mike Tyson and told him they would be putting in "a few screens and wide-outs" to capitalize on his broken-field running. He gave the team a pep talk. He told them now they had to prove they could win on the road, their next game being Saturday in Roanoke. Then he said, somewhat grimly, "Dave wants to talk to you."

They went deathly quiet as Ferrell held a stack of small manila envelopes in each hand. "The first thing I want to say to you is that the team is not going to fold. We lost in the neighborhood of eighteen thousand dollars. We're still working on finding jobs. We're working on finding some player sponsors where a fan helps out a player each week. But once again I want to tell you that the team is *not* going to fold." He cleared his throat and waggled the envelopes. "There is twelve dollars in cash in each of these envelopes. After the game Saturday you'll see another thirteen dollars." There was no particular reaction from the players. "I'm sorry, truly sorry," Ferrell said. "And I'm proud of you."

Ferrell turned it back over to Warwick, who diagrammed a couple of new plays and covered some minor pieces of business. "All right, remember, when we yell 'Purple,' it's an automatic three receivers." Heads nodded. "Oh, yeah, by the way," he said, almost as an afterthought, "there's a local civic group throwing a Rockets Night dinner and we need twelve volunteers. Show up, get a free meal." Hands shot up like Roman candles. "Okay, let's go," Warwick said, ready to lead them out of the catacombs and onto the practice field. "Give us twelve dollars' worth." And off to work they went, those sad young men.

The saddest story of all was that of Mike Tyson. Born out of wedlock twenty-seven years earlier, Tyson was raised by his maternal grandparents in a rough area of Charleston called Groggy Hill, the sort of place it seems he has always called home, a ghetto rife with poverty and drinking and drugs and general mayhem up to and including murder. But he discovered the one thing he could do better than anyone else was run like a frightened rabbit trapped in a box canyon ("In Groggy Hill you *better* be able to run"). Soon he became a three-sports star at Charleston High and, after three sensational football seasons there, it appeared he had a future. "I drooled over Mike Tyson for three years when I was coaching at West Virginia," says Bobby Bowden, by now head coach at Florida State. "But if I don't get a recommendation from a kid's coach I drop him. The coach said Mike was trouble."

The trouble came quite naturally. "I was running around with a lot of roughnecks," said Tyson. "We didn't have gangs and fighting and shooting, you know, it was just peer-group action. We'd get a little wine and beer, you know, and we'd party and have a lot of music and noise and, well, indulge. Some of 'em could be playing pro ball right now, but most of 'em are either on the streets or in jail or dead." He and the football coach had a falling out, so Mike devoted his senior year to track. He ran a 21-second 220 and a 9.5-second 100 and long-jumped 25 feet and began dreaming of the Olympics.

In the meantime Iowa State, a Big Eight football factory, took the gamble and gave him a football scholarship. In a four-minute span during one game of his freshman year he gained one hundred yards rushing. "I had a big sophomore pre-season, too," he said. "I didn't go out, didn't mess with no women. It was books and football." But his girlfriend was back home in Charleston with their baby daughter, and he couldn't take the separation. "If I'd had that solidity and calm, you know, I could have done the same thing Tony Dorsett did. I'd maybe be retired from the NFL already. But I had the little girl and I wanted her to have a father figure, something I never had, and kids just got to have that."

So once again Mike Tyson, whose troubles seem to amass as quickly as he can hit a tape or a goal line, packed it in and went back home. This was in 1975, when he was twenty, and the ensuing years became a scramble. In '78 the Dallas Cowboys paid his way out for an ill-fated tryout. The Winnipeg Bluebirds of the Canadian Football League gave him a quick look as a defensive back. He knocked around with various AFA teams, quitting one when they jumped him for nearly missing a plane. Then, finally, in the prelude to the 1980 Olympics, came the cruelest blow of all.

Qualifying for the United States Olympic track team involves an arduous series of competitions all over the country. Tyson had worked diligently for it. He was clean, had stuck around the house and trained for the trials. He had his times down to 10.1 for the 100 meters and 24.2 for the 220 meters. Then he went on the road and began outrunning the favorites like Houston McTeer and Harvey Glance and Dwight Evans. He had qualified for the second round in the 220 and when he flew out of the gate even he couldn't believe what was happening. "Here was this little boy from West Virginia nobody'd heard of and I was twenty yards ahead of 'em all." But twenty yards from the finish line he pulled up with a hamstring injury and couldn't finish the race. "I could've made the United States Olympic team. It hurt my heart."

Now, at twenty-seven, he was down to returning kicks in the AFA. He and his girlfriend had four kids at home by now and another farmed out to his grandmother. His daily routine included getting the kids ready for school, washing dishes and getting rid of the garbage while she was at work, jogging three or four miles, working with weights, looking for a job and, around five o'clock in the afternoon, finding a way to get to Laidley Field for practice. (His mind was more on the '84 Olympics trials, it seemed, but on another hot afternoon in Charleston as he sat in a motel coffee shop there were other things haunting Mike Tyson.) He is an extremely religious man, his mother and sister being Holiness preachers and his father a gospel singer, which explained why there were no scars on his knees from running with footballs for half his life: "We don't believe in surgery. We believe in prayer and faith healing."

He seems resigned to failure. "Olympics," he said, "that's my last chance. I know that. Everybody knows that. I've managed to mess up a lot in my life. If I'd gone on back to college it'd be different. But it was the kids. The kids." He still sees his own father around town, "but it's to the point where when I run into him on the street I don't know whether to call him Dad or Tyson or Raymond or just say, 'Hey, what's happening?' So I just say, 'Mikey misses you.' Life gets confusing sometimes."

And so, from that bleak day of the twelve-dollar envelopes, the embattled warriors of Stalag Thirteen and other crannies strung out along the Kanawha River valley slogged into summer. First they held a meeting with Ferrell and demanded that he not tell the media how little money they were getting because it was embarrassing. Then they got on a bus at eleven o'clock in the morning on the second Saturday of the season and took their pre-game meal at a restaurant near the stadium in Roanoke, went through the ritual of taping and suiting up, took out their frustrations on the hapless Roanoke Valley Express (51–7), fought over which beer was whose on the ride back to Charleston, plopped exhausted atop their beds at daybreak and looked forward to Tuesday when they would see the other half of their opening-game pittance. The next two games were back home at Laidley Field, where Ferrell hoped to begin recouping his opening-night loss, but again the rains were waiting for them. They slipped past the Canton Bulldogs, 24–17, and were surprised to see 1,728 fans bring their umbrellas and their money. Now they were getting $28 a week. Ferrell trimmed back ticket prices to entice bigger crowds. Game Four saw more rain but more fans (1,923) and another victory. The Rockets were 4–0 and holding.

To that point only Eric Hegrenes, the one who got on his motorbike and fled home to St. Paul after the opener, had found it unbearable. One by one they were finding menial jobs here and there. Some of them, even upon getting steady work, stayed on at Stalag because, as one of them said, "after a while it sort of grows on you." And, inevitably, injuries began to hit the team. Quarterback Steve Turk was paying for the inadequacies of his offensive line with a back pained from repeated muggings by pass rushers. As a consequence his backup, Steve Smith, was getting more playing time than he had bargained for; but then Smith had his arm broken by those same invaders and Turk, after staying up all night guarding the dump, had the additional duty of carrying the team on a back that wouldn't straighten. But that fourth game had dealt a luckless hand—to the man and to the team. On his first carry of the game, Mike Tyson took the handoff and went flying into the masses and didn't get up. It was the knee. In three games he had returned five kickoffs for 285 yards and three touchdowns, run back seven punts for 118 yards and two scores, and rushed 16 times for 112 yards and one touchdown. That meant he had laid his hands on the football 28 times for 515 yards (an average of 18.4 yards) and six touchdowns. He was the fire behind the Rockets, the game-breaker, the untouchable blur. And now Mike Tyson was gone from football, perhaps forever.

The first loss came in game five, up in Racine to the eventual AFA champion Wisconsin Gladiators. They had whipped Virginia at home in more rain, lost at Canton, and drew 1,441 for an exhibition game at Laidley (kids with an adult were charged a penny for admission) before closing out the regular season in a somewhat heady manner. The night of July 24th was marked by high cobalt skies for the first time all summer, and 6,444 fans saw the Rockets lose to Wisconsin on the last series of downs. The following week 4,365 sat through a slight rain to see their boys whip Buffalo in overtime and make the AFA playoff with a 7–3 record.

But that, except for a couple of lively flurries which kept them on the sports pages for a few extra days, was it for the 1982 Charleston Rockets. On the first day of practice for the opening playoff game the players went on strike when they found out Ferrell had been selling tickets for one dollar each to businesses buying them in blocks of fifty. And there was the hare-brained idea of paying Kenny Stabler five thousand dollars to come out of retirement if Charleston and Wisconsin were paired in the second round at Laidley Field. (The plot was rendered moot when the Carolina Storm blew the Rockets out, 63–13.) So it was over. The club wound up averaging 2,795 in paid attendance, leaving Ferrell with about a $10,000 loss (none of the surviving sixteen AFA teams broke even), and each of the thirty-seven Rockets made between $500 and $600 for playing fourteen games. Terry Rusin, the survivor, had four interceptions and one fumble recovery and eight blocked passes and thirty-three individual tackles for the season. Lonnie Warwick still held to his dream of maybe catching on as an assistant in the new United States Football League. The only Rocket to get a shot in the NFL was Larry Delwiche, the punter, who made it to the final cut at the Chicago Bears' camp. Some of the players planned to stick around and play in a new six-team Ohio Football League, at a flat rate of fifty dollars per game, but for the bulk of them it was time to go home. Home, where the rainbow began. They were still trying to find the end of it.

Goodlife, 1985

9

It's a Mad, Mad, Mad Whirl

IT IS FIVE DEGREES BELOW zero on a Saturday night in mid-January, but nobody inside the cavernous Cincinnati Gardens is thinking about that right now because the Roller Derby has come to town. Down on the portable banked track the ladies of the Pioneers and the ladies of the Bombers have already bent themselves to the business of trying to kill each other off in the first "game" of a doubleheader. Elbows are flying, skates are clacking, fans are screaming for blood, and all of it is being orchestrated by a hysterical trackside announcer who sounds a lot like Howard Cosell: *Weston coming up on the outside, Forbes with a blow to the head of Tucker. . . . Twenty seconds to go, Bombers lead by two. . . . Forbes forms a whip, starting the play. . . . Eight seconds, eight seconds left. . . . Here's Garello, Garello SCOORES!* Pandemonium. Everybody up. *Official decision, two Pioneer points. Tie game! Tie game!* Unable to contain herself any longer, a lady in pink doubleknit toreador pants and blue hair charges the lip of the track and pastes little Jackie Garello in the left breast with a rolled-up Dixie cup.

Charlie Knuckles is watching the games this night with considerable interest. Five days from now he will take a plane to the West Coast and enroll in the official Roller Derby training school. With a name like this they can make him a star. A slight eighteen-year-old with shaggy unkempt hair and a pimply face, he made the big decision as soon as he got out of the Job Corps in October. He has been cleaning out condemned houses for a construction company, hoarding his money, and he has it all worked out: "It's just a buck a day for the school. You can live at the YMCA for four a day and a buddy told me you can pick up twenty-five or thirty bucks unloading a truck." The product of a broken home, never much interested in basic sports, he has been "messing around at little dinky rinks" since he was ten. In many ways he is typical of the Derby stars he has followed for nearly half his life.

"Yeah, I been planning this a long time," he says as the period ends and the male Bombers and Pioneers take over the track. "I'm on their mailing list, watch 'em on TV, even hitchhiked to Cleveland to see 'em once. Ain't never smoked. Got my knee busted speed-skating one time and took walks in the hospital at three o'clock in the morning to strengthen it. You know, build it back up."

"Never skated a banked track, then?" somebody asked.

"Naw. That's what the training school's for."

"How long does that take?"

"Depends. They gotta teach ya how to fall, how to block, how to jam. Some guys get signed up in a week. Others, they'll maybe get put on an amateur team for a while." Out on the track a Bomber is chasing a Pioneer through the infield with a metal folding chair. "Jesus, I hope he kills him."

"C'mon. You don't believe that."

Blinking incredulously, Charlie Knuckles doesn't bother to dignify that with a reply.

Essentially it is, as the title of a Derby-sponsored paperback reads, "a very simple game." Two teams of five players skate counterclockwise around a banked track, 310 feet in circumference, that can fit into a 50-by-90-foot rectangular space. Each team has two skaters at the rear of the pack called "jammers." When a jammer breaks through the pack, the countdown begins and the jammers have thirty seconds to lap the pack. Every time a jammer laps an opposing skater he scores a point for his team. There are certain finer points in the rule book, of course, but that's about the size of it. The Roller Derby isn't so much a sport as it is a caricature of sport—pure show business, a higher form of "Friday Night Rasslin'," pregnant with scowling villains and glamorous heroines pulling hair and cracking skulls almost every night inside some auditorium somewhere in a melodramatic morality play that sends thousands of proletarian fans into delirious frenzy. "I never heard them say, 'Tonight we win, tomorrow night you win,'" says author Frank Deford, who spent considerable time traveling with the Derby caravan for a book called *Five Strides on the Banked Track.* "But I never saw a lopsided game. There's almost an unwritten rule that you let up when you get 'way ahead. There are always bits of business to be done, like throwing a chair or sending [Ann] Calvello through somebody's legs or knocking over the water cooler. The hitting is seldom for real."

But never mind. There is a sizable underground in America that *wants* to believe in the Derby, just as it wants to believe in professional wrestling. This belief has made it one of the hottest entertainments going. Six teams play one-nighters on the road for seven straight months and are seen by more than three million paid customers. (Last year, when the Derby went into New York's Madison Square Garden for the first time, there were three consecutive sellouts.) A total of 132 television stations carry weekly syndicated taped Derby games. Upward of a thousand fan letters reach Derby headquarters in Oakland, California, each week. Every Monday an average of one hundred hopefuls like Charlie Knuckles check into the Derby training school, straining to find the brass ring. At least two movies, one of them starring Raquel Welch as the queen bee, were being made by major studios. Charlie O'Connell, the Derby's top drawing card, earns around $60,000 a year. The Bay Bombers franchise was recently sold to a Texas group for a reported $1 million. And Bay Promotions, Inc., the parent company for the entire operation (funded in the late 1950s with $500), last year grossed nearly $8 million. "Well, gee, let 'em go watch lacrosse," says Bay Promotions president Gerald E. Seltzer of purists who would scorn his game.

I am reminded of Cowboy Luttrell, whose company I shared when I was a young newspaper sports editor in Tampa, Florida, and he was the local wrestling mogul. A rollicking old codger who had lost one eye in an exhibition boxing match with Jack Dempsey, Cowboy was a fixture in steamy downtown Tampa, where he lived in a fading hotel and lunched in dark bars and terrified shoppers by lurching down Florida Avenue at high noon in his magnificent white shark-finned Cadillac.

Cowboy was your basic wrestling entrepreneur. He had a stable of athletes with outrageous pseudonyms like Klondike Bill and Kublah Khan, and on any night of the week they could be found practicing their vaudevillian routines in small-town auditoriums all over the northern stretches of Florida. Seldom was there anything short of a capacity crowd for their shows, no matter where or when they performed, bringing great wealth and a sort of underground celebrity to Cowboy and his men. Stuck deep in Cowboy's craw, however, was the fact that we gave the fuzzy Class A Tampa Tarpons baseball club top play almost daily while burying our scant mention of pro wrestling among the tire-recapping ads.

"Hey," he said one day while we fished the Gulf in his twenty-four-foot boat, "great story on us yesterday. Two paragraphs."

"Okay, Cowboy," I said.

"The Tarpons. What'd they draw?"

"You read. A hundred and twelve."

"My boys," he smiled, "four thousand. Power of the press, my ass."

Jerry Seltzer is a suave, forty-year-old Northwestern graduate who took over the business from his father, Leo, fourteen years ago when the Derby, badly overexposed nationally during the early days of television, was drawing crowds of two hundred at the Cow Palace in San Francisco. The Derby had sprung out of the walkathon and marathon bike-race crazes of the Depression years (indeed, such present-day Derby terms as "jamming" are holdovers). Leo Seltzer patiently nursed it into a popular, offbeat, and fairly legitimate sport until the honeymoon ended and he disgustedly turned the whole thing over to his only son. Jerry had been slogging along as a salesman, announcing Derby games for pocket money, and there wasn't much to recommend him as a savior except that he came armed with the instincts of a newer generation that had been teethed on television. He was wise enough to know that baseball, for one, was being killed by too much television and too much devotion to tradition. In 1960 people wanted action and the trick was to keep them hungering for it. Going on his instincts most of the way, Jerry Seltzer hit upon a formula that is a classic study in successful promotion.

On the surface it is difficult to comprehend that a venture could be so successful with virtually no help from the usual publicity sources, principally newspapers. "We asked the wire services if they would carry our standings this year. UPI said they ought to wait and see how it worked out. AP never answered," says Derby publicist Herb Michelson. On the day of most games in most towns there will be at best a three-paragraph mention of the Derby on the local sports page. Seltzer couldn't care less; he has gone straight to his audience, amassing a mailing list of 250,000 fans who regularly receive press releases about the league and when *their team* will next play in *their* area. The six Derby teams represent definite geographical areas; the Midwest Jolters, for example, are the "home" team when they play anywhere between Michigan and Kentucky.

Bay Promotions is a synergistic machine—it covers the Derby itself, the television syndicate, an ad agency, the training school, a skate factory, a publishing house, and a movie production company (whose *Derby* was rated by some critics as one of the top ten documentary films for 1971). "The San Francisco *Chronicle* runs a long boxing column once a week," says Michelson, "but what do we care? Boxing crowds in the Bay area average around 1,800 people, and everybody *knows* what we draw. We've got our own thing going." Indeed they do. On the night before the Cincinnati doubleheader, which drew more than 8,000 in subzero weather with only an obscure two-column newspaper ad, the National Basketball Association game between the Cincinnati Royals and the Atlanta Hawks enticed only 3,908, even with the help of a lead story on Friday's sports pages.

• • •

Like most of the Chiefs and Jolters, Ann Calvello and Margie Laszlo get away from Cincinnati by ten o'clock in the morning. That night the two teams will play at the Convention Center in Louisville and Ann and Margie want to reach the downtown Holiday Inn in time to watch the Super Bowl (and the Roller Derby tape) on color television. Calvello, who signs her autograph just that way, is forty-three years old and tired of traveling. Laszlo, already a veteran of thirteen years with the Derby, is twenty-nine and would like to get married. Bushed from five straight nights of skating in five separate towns—not to mention a hard Saturday night of carousing in Cincinnati—Calvello has turned her car over to somebody else (its special California license plate reads L-O-V-E-R) so she can catch up on her sleep. Before the season ends in April, they will have driven nearly fifty thousand miles. Laszlo tanks up at a gas station, meticulously records her mileage in a black diary, then heads out to the southbound interstate highway.

There are roughly one hundred skaters employed by the Roller Derby, half of them women, a third of them black (black fans tend to huddle together in small knots during road dates). Even though a lot of ink is given to O'Connell's $60,000 salary and statuesque Joan Weston's $50,000 (Calvello is the third highest-paid at around $35,000), rookies begin at $8,000 and the great bulk of them earn in the teens. The *Roller Derby Yearbook* has fascinating things to say about them all—"Won't back down from a battle," "Has a variety of often-painful crunching moves"—but the truth is that the average skater comes from a tumultuous lower-class background, wasn't much at other sports, has little education and is painfully shy when off the track. "Most of us are pretty quiet and I guess it is a release to get out on the track," says one demure female skater. There is some homosexuality, male and female, but not much. There is usually at least one flaming love affair taking place on each tour, especially when some young stud has just joined the troupe. About a third of the men have nonskating wives back home and there are but four married skating couples on the road. For most the Derby is an endless cycle—skate, drive four hundred miles, catch a nap in a motel, skate, move out again—that leaves little time for hobbies or marriage or thinking beyond next week. Few skaters stay at it for more than four or five years. "The road, that's what gets to you," says Calvello. "I had a week off at Christmas, but it wasn't worth it to go all the way to the Coast. Me, I spent Christmas at a Holiday Inn in Chicago."

There has been but one death on the track in Derby history, but only two survived a massive bus accident in the 1930s and several others have died or been ruined on the open road. Traveling is especially hazardous now that the season runs from October through April. "One time it took us five hours to make the hundred and twenty miles from Saginaw to Battle Creek," recalls Laszlo. And what happened once in a thirty-five-below night in Canada isn't entirely out of the ordinary: the rental truck carrying the portable track (the Derby keeps eight of them in circulation) got snowbound, there was a sellout crowd waiting, and the skaters turned down the frantic promoter's suggestion to "just draw a track on the floor" of the gymnasium and skate. "When I started out I was making forty dollars a month, plus room and board," says Calvello. "Now I've got a phone bill of a hundred and fifty a month, just calling my daughter."

Ann Calvello is a story to herself. The oldest of a sailor's six kids, she joined the Derby in 1948 and is one of only eighteen members of the Derby Hall of Fame. Unlike most of the female skaters, she is an extrovert—an astrology buff, a friend of Bay Area professional athletes, a born villainess ("I don't want to be a cigarette," meaning one content to "sit back in the pack"), a walking commercial for Roller Derby (featured in a Public Television *Great American Dream Machine* spot on the Derby) and an expert on everything ("What's wrong with this generation is they got no discipline. I saw a guy yesterday eating a salad with his hands"). She has had raging affairs with more than one Derby star but now goes with a San Francisco fireman. She and her teenage daughter share an apartment featuring a psychedelic toilet. The constant traveling and skating have taken her looks—she has gone through broken noses, stitched eyes and torn lips, and wears braces on both knees—but she is still the most singular figure in the game with her blond polka-dot hair (sprayed on by Margie Laszlo before each game) and an animated face bursting with freckles.

"Ahh, sometimes I think it's no life for a girl," Calvello is saying as we reach the outskirts of Louisville. She is sprawled over the front seat in flowery bell-bottoms and a Notre Dame jacket and scruffy brown Hush Puppies. "You come back off the road and find yourself opening car doors for men. I have to remember to act helpless."

"I may have to get a divorce before I get married," says Laszlo. "I've been going with this one guy since I was sixteen."

"Hey," says Calvello. "You know that movie Raquel is doing?"

"The Derby movie?"

"Right. Well, I want to tell you that she's actually playing me. *Calvello.* How 'bout that? She may have bigger tickets [Derby slang for breasts] than me, but I can outskate her."

Another day, another town. If it's Sunday, this must be Louisville. They played here two weeks earlier, celebrating New Year's Eve by running up and down the streets at midnight outside a crummy little beer joint on a lonely street, and here they are again. The crew of younger skaters goes out in mid-afternoon to assemble the track (for three hours' work, putting it up and taking it down, a man earns around thirty dollars) while the others crawl in bed and watch the Super Bowl from New Orleans. There is that familiar two-column ad on the sports page of the Louisville *Courier-Journal,* plus a slightly longer story because one of the Derby rookies hails from Louisville, and then there will be the Derby on television later in the day. As in Detroit and Fort Wayne and Cincinnati, a poster outside the Louisville Convention Center reminds fans to come and see "Your Jolters" do battle.

Joan Weston and Ann Calvello are big, but nobody in the game is as big as Charlie O'Connell. At the heart of Roller Derby is the ability to play a part, to lull the crowd into a never-never land of good guys and bad guys—in short, to make them either love you or hate you—and nobody can anger a crowd like "Bomber Great Charlie O'Connell," as the press releases always call him. He is the classic heavy: big for a skater (six-foot-two,

two hundred pounds), moody and sullen, sort of a malevolent John Wayne on wheels. He has the crowd on his back the moment he rolls out for warmups with a white towel tucked tightly around his neck and stuffed into his jacket collar like a prizefighter. He is No. 40, an All-Star every year since 1958 and the only other active skater besides Calvello who is in the Hall of Fame.

O'Connell represents one case where no flackery is needed. He is truly a villain, not only with the fans but with many of the skaters and the people back in the front office at Oakland. They refer to him there as "GSB," which stands for "Greedy Son-of-a-Bitch." He stays to himself on most of the tour, most of the time bringing along his wife. While almost all of the skaters live on the West Coast, and O'Connell himself has a spacious home overlooking the Bay Area, he now prefers living in a suburban community an hour north of New York City. He got burned on a couple of investments in bars and restaurants and now simply puts his $60,000 a year in the bank and lives the good life when not on the road. He has come a long way. He grew up poor on Manhattan's Lower East Side and says most of his boyhood pals are "on one side of the law or the other" today.

Tonight, in Louisville, O'Connell is not in a good mood. He was late getting into town and as soon as this engagement is over he and his wife will have to drive five hundred miles straight to Springfield, Missouri. At 36, he is suffering injuries more regularly. He has just returned from a five-month layoff due to a broken forearm and is surlier and fifteen pounds heavier than usual. He thinks he just might quit all this stuff.

"Hell, I'm skating against twenty-year-old kids now," he says. He is sitting in a narrow hallway outside the dressing room. The game has already started, ladies first, and you can hear the bellowing of the crowd through the heavily guarded door.

"What would you do if you quit?"

"Coach, I guess. Hell, I'd like to be one of them rich landlords, to tell the truth. Anything but working."

"You wouldn't miss skating, then?"

"Yeah, I'd miss it." He wraps the towel around his neck and crosses his legs. "Stuff gets into your blood. I tried to quit once and about went nuts. I can honestly say I'd be in a hell of a fix if it hadn't been for skating."

"What do you say to people who call the Derby phony?"

He spins a wheel on one of his skates. "They're crazy."

"It's all on the up-and-up, then?"

"Naw. Look. What about Ted Williams? There was a great athlete, but do you think he'd have made all that money if he hadn't been a little something extra? I mean like giving people the finger and spitting toward the press box? Hell, there's a little bit of show business in everything. Okay, we have a little fun now and then. I'll tell you one thing, though. This damn broken arm ain't no put-on."

Having spoken thus, "Bomber Great Charlie O'Connell" pushes the door aside and skates across the broad expanse of concrete to the banked track. Although the girls are still whirling around, all eyes turn to him and the auditorium reverberates with boos and cheers. He gives them their money's worth. In the first minute of play he belts a black Jolter with a forearm chop, showing princely disdain as the skater flies all the way over the cushioned rail and sprawls out cold on the slick concrete floor. As the first half ends, O'Connell is sitting out his second one-minute penalty and an out-and-out brawl breaks out in the infield. *Both coaches are fined $100! Both coaches are fined $100!* the announcer keeps shouting above the roar of the crowd. Nobody hears him because the same black Jolter is taking a folding chair over the head this time, cops are trying to head off the hundred or so fans swarming down onto the track, and both teams are bursting through for the dressing room. When Charlie is twenty feet from the door a pretty girl in yellow stretch pants comes running up to him and—thinking the vilest of thoughts—rears back and unloads a full cup of chipped ice right in his face. "Bomber Great Charlie O'Connell" smiles benevolently at her before going on inside to see how badly he hurt the guy.

True, 1972

We Were Champions, Once

DURING THE 1950S, THE CITY of Auburn, Alabama, didn't vary much from the other small towns in the South whose principal industry was a college. Starkville and Clemson and Auburn were pretty much the same. Suspended out there on the high rolling farm-pond plains of east Alabama—"Auburn, Loveliest Village of the Plain," it called itself, from the Goldsmith poem—the town's rhythms were more or less determined by the students of what was then known as Alabama Polytechnic Institute, "dear old API" of the school song. The resident population nearly doubled when school was in session, and on football Saturdays little Auburn became the fifth-largest city in the state.

All of the trappings of a university town were there. You could tell the time of day by glancing up at the clock tower atop old Samford Hall, visible from nearly everywhere. You bought your books or calculators or your Auburn souvenirs—anything from T-shirts to beer mugs, as long as it came in orange-and-blue, the school colors—at Johnston-Malone on College Avenue. You could shoot pool down toward the Opelika Highway, just before the railroad tracks, and you could get drunk and play country music on the jukebox at an enormous beer joint on the old Montgomery Highway called The Casino. You snuggled up with your date at a movie theater, the War Eagle, in the center of downtown. You structured your fall social season around the schedule of the Auburn Tigers (or, variously, the War Eagles or the Plainsmen). Early on, as a freshman being forced to wear a stupid beanie cap, you learned the Auburn war cry, a full-throated scream not unlike a Rebel Yell: *Waaaar EA-gul!*

In 1957, the last year the college would be known officially as Alabama Polytechnic Institute, Auburn was still thought of as the state's "cow college." Founded on the eve of the Civil War as a land-grant institution, first as East Alabama Male College and then as Alabama Agricultural and Mechanical, the school had always specialized in engineering and agriculture. Peopled by the sons of farmers, or young men who had a knack for building things like roads and bridges and barns, Auburn always had a bucolic, masculine feel. It was a place where a country boy, the first in his family's history to attend college, could survive, even feel at home, as he trod the dirt paths connecting the old red brick buildings on the campus. Small-town girls from all over the state knew that, too, saw Auburn as a good place to go in search of what they called an "MRS Degree," and so they swarmed in from Dadeville and Eufaula and Andalusia, majoring in Home Economics for the most part, giving Auburn a five-to-one ratio of male to female students.

It was known as a friendly place, one of modest aspirations, a springboard to a good job and a lasting marriage. Except for a group of men enrolled in the school of aeronautical engineering, soon to find themselves thrust into the middle of the space race against the Soviet Union as astronauts and flight engineers, Auburn students didn't concern themselves very much with events beyond the state of Alabama. They would let others harbor dreams of making it in New York City or conquering new worlds in California. Auburn men of that time were content to build better roads and bridges at home, to open an apothecary or become a veterinarian in their hometowns, to go their farming daddies one step better by becoming an agricultural advisor, or to move from the factory floor to the rooms where corporate decisions are made.

Any pressures Auburn people felt in those days emanated from across the state, at the University of Alabama in Tuscaloosa. Ever since its inception as the university in the state, Alabama's role had been to produce lawyers, doctors, educators, bankers, and thus potential executives and political leaders. This left Auburn, little API, as a clear underdog in many ways: in political clout, in alumni endowments, in public perception. You could visit most of the small towns all across the state and find out very quickly who held the real power: graduates of the University of Alabama, the doctors and lawyers, men of wealth and position—not Auburn people, the veterinarians and engineers and agricultural extension agents and homemakers and nurses, albeit *agreeable* law-abiding citizens of good heart, but nevertheless people with little real clout. Thus, in the public eye, Auburn continued to be known as the state's "cow college."

Naturally, in a state where football might as well be sanctioned as a religion, this perception extended to the football field. While it's true that Auburn had enjoyed moments of success during its infancy (an early coach was John Heisman, for whom the Heisman Trophy was named), the mighty Alabama Crimson Tide had been a national powerhouse for most of the first half of the twentieth century. Auburn had played in only one post-season bowl game of importance, a visit to the Orange Bowl during the Depression, but Alabama had been to the Rose Bowl six times and in between trips to Pasadena was a regular in the Sugar, Cotton, and Orange bowls. The reason was simple. When a genuine football prospect came along and had to choose where he would go to play his college ball—*What'll it be, son, Alabama or Auburn?*—it was no contest. The Auburn alumni in town, the vet and the druggist and the extension agent, didn't have a prayer against the doctor and the lawyer and the mayor when it came to recruiting the young player and sending him off to Tuscaloosa for four years.

Thus, there sprouted a body of cruel "Auburn jokes" designed to intensify an Auburn man's inferiority complex. The best thing to ever come out of Auburn? *Interstate 85.* How'd you know I'm an Auburn man? *I noticed your ring while you were picking your nose.* Take any Polish joke, it becomes an Auburn joke. *A blonde at a bar tells the Auburn man trying to pick her up that she's a lesbian; unfazed, he asks her how things are going in Beirut.* Later, when Bear Bryant returned to his alma mater and thoroughly dominated the Alabama-Auburn series, Auburn fans could only meekly retaliate with Bear jokes of their own. *Fishing from a boat with Shug Jordan* [Auburn's coach], *Bear falls into the water and Shug saves him from drowning. Bear asks Shug not to let people find out he can't actually walk on water. Shug says okay, if you won't let my people know I saved you.* And this, when Bryant failed to win in eight straight bowl games: *When a waitress asks Bear how he wants his soup, he says better make it a cup, I can't handle a bowl.* It was weak stuff, and the only real retaliation would come with a championship team of their own.

In the waning days of August in 1957, the football players began drifting back to Auburn from their homes all across the state, about a hundred of them in all, to check into a rambling collection of white-frame cottages known as Graves Center. They were unheralded country boys, for the most part, fitting the Auburn mold, and only the coaches were there to greet them. They parked their rumpled cars and pickup trucks beneath the pines before any of the other students had arrived, tossed their belongings into their assigned cabins, swapped tales of summer jobs and fleeting romances, and then plunged into the business of checking in for another football season: enrolling in classes, taking physical examinations, being fitted for everything from jockstraps to shoulder pads, receiving play books, and learning when Hoot Gibson, the sprightly woman who served as "athletic dietician," would be serving meals at the barracks-style mess hall. So began the unlikely odyssey of the boys who would become the best college football team in America by the time the grass turned brown in December.

There was little tradition to Auburn football that would presage what was about to happen that year. The school had fielded its first team in 1892, coached by a Dr. George Petrie, and that first team split four games but was outscored by 98 points to 42. Now and then there would be a splendid season, as in 1900 when the team went 4–0 and outscored its opponents, 148–5. John Heisman had coached there for the last five years of the 1800s. Later coaches like Mike Donahue and Jack Meagher were still being lionized. The 1937 team had laid a 6–0 shutout on Michigan State in the Orange Bowl. But in the turn-of-the-century years Auburn football was not unlike the sort of life API's future farmers would soon be facing in the real world: one year of plenty, followed by four years of drought.

In 1950, the bottom fell out. Auburn began that season by losing to Wofford at home by a score of 19–14 and ended it with a 30–0 blowout at the hands of hated Alabama at Legion Field in Birmingham. A somewhat disorganized coach by the name of Earl Brown was canned after winning only three games in three years. The search was on for a new coach to lead Auburn into the '50s, but not many of the candidates were bothering to return calls to this little country school stuck out there somewhere between Montgomery and Columbus, Georgia. Auburn's stadium had just 18,000 seats, no more than 10,000 of them being filled on Saturdays, they had lost not only to Wofford but to Southeastern Louisiana as well, and the athletic program was $75,000 in debt.

Then one day when panic was setting in, a simple handwritten note reached the Auburn athletic department, postmarked at the University of Georgia in Athens. It was from a former three-sports star, an Auburn man, then an assistant coach at Georgia. "I hereby apply for the position of head football coach at Auburn," the note read, followed by a somewhat petulant postscript: "If you don't believe in Auburn people, you ought to close the place down." It was signed by one Ralph Jordan.

Conservative, unassuming, businesslike, Ralph Jordan seemed to be the quintessential Auburn man. He and Jeff Beard, the Auburn athletic director who had pushed Jordan into writing the note in the first place, were both sons of the soil, the rich Black Belt that stretches across the midsection of Alabama. (Beard loved to tell the story of how his brother, Percy, won medals at the 1932 Olympics in Los Angeles and came back home to Pine Apple, Alabama, to find only a mention of his heroics in the county's weekly newspaper: "Percy Beard has returned from California, where he participated in a footrace.") Ralph "Shug" Jordan—his nickname came from his affinity for sugar cane as a barefoot lad in Selma—had come from a world where a man marries for life, takes a nap at noon, treats his neighbors like family, drives the same car until it dies, and more or less does the best he can with the cards he has been dealt. Like Beard with his story about brother Percy, Jordan was self-effacing; *his* favorite story was about how he, as a stumpy left-handed pitcher at Auburn, had thrown his high hard one only to have the batter catch it barehanded and throw it back. Auburn and Shug Jordan, then, seemed to be a perfect match.

But Auburn football was absolutely bankrupt, in more ways than one, when Jordan took over prior to the 1951 season. The debilitating Korean War was running in full agony, taking most of the able men halfway around the world. The good ones were playing at Tennessee and Alabama and Georgia, anywhere but Auburn, and the famous Auburn Spirit was on vacation, awaiting further developments. Desperate times called for desperate measures, and there are survivors of the '51 preseason camp who still cringe at the memory. Jordan opened it to anybody who was ambulatory—battle-scarred Korean veterans on the G.I. Bill, 4-Fs, raw teenagers sought by no one—and the blood of more than a hundred applicants ran freely on the practice fields. "When it's broke, fix it," was another of Shug Jordan's homilies. Auburn somehow finished with a 5–5 record that year (losing to Alabama again, 25–7), and after a more thorough housecleaning the Tigers went 2–8 in '52.

In a state the size of Alabama there is only so much talent to go around, and seldom has it happened that both Alabama and Auburn have been at the top of their game at the same time. The pendulum is always swinging back and forth; when Alabama is getting most of the prime beef in a prime-beef state, Auburn is down, and vice versa. By the early- to mid-'50s, two things were happening to swing the pendulum in Auburn's favor: Alabama was paying for a poor selection of a head coach, J. B. "Ears" Whitworth, whose first team went 0–10, and Shug Jordan's rebuilding program was showing promise to any high school prospect who wanted to play on a winning team. Auburn steamrolled Alabama in the big game at Legion Field for the three straight years prior to 1957—by scores of 28–0, 26–0, and 34–7—and obviously the pendulum had swung again in Auburn's favor after too many years of second-class citizenship. Beginning with the 1953 team, Jordan's third, Auburn went to the Gator Bowl for three consecutive years, and was headed for an even bigger bowl game in '56 until disaster struck: they were put on probation by the National Collegiate Athletic Association, for overzealous recruiting.

There were back-to-back probations, in fact, that would haunt the players gathering for the '57 preseason practice during the rest of their days. First, there had been "illegal inducements" to sign a heralded quarterback from Huntsville by the name of Don Fuell—a window air-conditioning unit here, use of a fishing boat there—and then an assistant coach foolishly wrote out checks to a pair of twin brothers from Gadsden, hotshot running backs known as the Beaube Twins, whose father was a preacher and whose high school coach was an Alabama man. It was the ultimate paper trail, leading to two more years of probation tacked on to the Fuell penalty. (On top of that, the school of engineering had lost its accreditation due to overburdened classrooms.) At some point in there, an anguished homemade poster was seen nailed to a telephone pole on College Avenue in downtown Auburn: *Auburn Gives the World 24 Hours to Get out of Town.*

And there was more, the boys of 1957 would learn as they checked into Graves Center for the preseason in August of that year. During summer school, two of their starters, quarterback Jimmy Cook and fullback Donnie May, had been dismissed from the team for taking beer into a women's dorm and generally misbehaving. And now they were hearing rumors that a promising running back, Bobby Hoppe, who once whiled away lazy spring afternoons in Graves Center by shooting pine cones out of the trees with a .45 pistol, was being detained back home in Chattanooga in a fatal shooting. Whatever the deal was, Hoppe hadn't yet arrived, if he would at all, and Cook and May were history. Some writers were picking Auburn to finish no better than fifth in the Southeastern Conference, the Dixie Dozen, and now the heart of the offense was gone. What next?

To find out, they gathered in an amphitheater beneath a grove of pines in Graves Center, wearing summer tans and Bermuda shorts and worried looks, to hear Shug address the situation. He spoke to them as a grandfather, wrinkling his brow, pursing his lips, evenly and firmly. "I know letting Jimmy and Donnie go doesn't sound good, but it had to be done, and it's all over," he said. "Down through the years, we here at Auburn have been accustomed to adversity"—no specific mention here of having shot itself in the foot with the NCAA probation—"and we've become stronger for it. You all appear to be in good shape. You're Auburn men. You're going to work hard and work together, and we're going to make ourselves proud of what happens this year."

There was much cheering and bravado, but that cooled quickly. "Our fullback will be Billy Atkins," Jordan said, "and our quarterback will be Lloyd Nix." What? *Nix?* Billy Atkins they could see—he was a senior who could run, block, and placekick—but Lloyd Nix had been a third-string halfback the year before, running the ball only thirty times, a left-hander who hadn't played quarterback since high school and had thrown exactly one pass as a halfback at Auburn. He had better be good to make them forget last year's starter, Howell Tubbs (grizzled, hard-nosed, averaged better than four yards a carry and completed more than half his passes), and his heir apparent, Jimmy Cook (22-for-40 passing, averaged 3.7 yards rushing). They knew Lloyd to be a good guy—from the little town of Kansas, west of Birmingham, studied all the time, wanted to be a dentist, dated a campus beauty—but, hey, he lobbed wobbly passes and still wore 44, a halfback number.

Jordan knew exactly what he was doing, as it would turn out, and in due time, as they continued drilling in the grueling heat of late-summer Alabama, they began to get the message. Lacking the guns for a high-powered offense, but loaded with hard-nosed country boys who could tear your head off if riled, they would play defense. They would hold onto the ball, play safety first, manage just enough first downs on the ground to maintain possession, win the kicking game, and force mistakes by the opposition. And picking Lloyd Nix as his quarterback was genius; he had the perfect temperament to run a cautious no-frills offense, to steer a ship around dangerous shoals. Those daily practices during the preseason turned out to be as hellish as the ones preceding Jordan's first year, fraught with fist-fights and middle-aged coaches down in the pits with the boys, shouting and cajoling and cursing, their voices ringing throughout the quiet little campus: "Dammit, Powell, the only good thing about you ran down yo' mama's leg!" "Don't *kiss* him, LaRussa, *kill* him!" It got so that they prayed for the season to begin so they could take a break.

To play a football game against the University of Tennessee at the cavernous Neyland Stadium in Knoxville can be a terrifying experience. UT fans show up the night before, the fat cats among them anchoring their yachts in the Tennessee River just beyond one end zone and partying through the evening with mash whiskey and country-music stars on board, and they take to the Saturday pursuit of the enemy much like a hound dog chases a 'coon. Intimidation is their mantra as they recount the exploits of the famous Big Orange heroes of the past: General Robert Neyland, Beattie Feathers, Bob Suffridge, George Cafego, Hank Lauricella, Johnny Majors. It was Majors, in fact, who in 1956 at Legion Field in Birmingham had held the last major symposium on how to properly operate the single-wing offense. The Volunteers beat Auburn terribly, by a score of 35–7.

Now, in 1957, here came the same Auburn team, minus its two big guns (Bobby Hoppe had finally checked in, whatever the deal was about the man he was alleged to have killed), trotting out onto Neyland in their unfamiliar whites against the UT Vols in their classic orange jerseys with some fifty thousand crazies up there swigging Jack Daniels in a drenching downpour. Back then, every player went both ways, offense and defense, and it was only about that time that they had begun to wear protective face masks (actually, a single Plexiglass strip on the helmet around the area of the nose). Shug Jordan was employing a two-team system—one unit would go ten minutes both ways and then the other would take over for the next ten minutes, no matter what happened—in order to keep fresh troops on the field. It was not uncommon in those days for college football players to spend up to fifty minutes on the field.

So Auburn and Tennessee stomped and cursed and sludged through the mud of Neyland Stadium for more than two hours, and Jordan's system prevailed. *You win by not losing.* Auburn won the toss and elected to receive and drove all the way to the UT two-yard-line but couldn't score. Later, the Tigers missed a field goal. They were punching away, but they couldn't score. Then, to begin the second quarter, a big end named Jerry Wilson partially blocked a punt, and Auburn took over on its 43 and began to move on the muddy ground. They reached the Tennessee five. There was a give to halfback Tommy Lorino and then three straight handoffs to Billy Atkins. On the last, Atkins dove into the end zone. His extra-point kick made it 7–0 Auburn, and the lead held. Tennessee's crushing single-wing offense netted only seventy yards in forty-one tries on the ground, and the Vols were held to minus yardage overall.

A curious thing happened on Sunday morning. *The New York Times* ran a rare eight-column headline on the sports page: "Auburn Marches 57 Yards in Second Quarter to Conquer Tennessee Eleven." Now, Auburn was in business. Tennessee had been a heavy favorite, but Auburn had shut them down right there in Knoxville. A "cow college," indeed. Auburn massacred little Chattanooga at home the next week, 40–7, and ran up a score of 48–7 a few weeks later at Houston, but for the most part they were winning, week after week, by shutting down the opposition and scoring just enough to prevail. They beat Georgia Tech 3–0, Kentucky 6–0, Florida 13–0. Their only scare came in Birmingham when they left Legion Field at halftime, behind for the first time all season. Mississippi State led 7–0, and Shug Jordan saw no need for hysterics; he told them they were the best and he loved them, and if they played their game they would win this one. They took the kickoff to open the second half and began to grind away on the ground behind all of those malevolent country boys on the offensive line. In the huddle, somewhere around the Mississippi State twenty-yard line, Hoppe snarled at Nix—"Gimme the damned ball and I'll score"—and that's exactly what happened. When it was over, Auburn had won, 15–7.

During the three-hour bus ride back home to Auburn, where they were greeted with a wild celebration at Toomer's Corner, at the center of town, somebody heard on the radio that top-rated Oklahoma had been defeated. Now Auburn, with a 7–0 record, was three steps away from the NCAA championship. Their remaining games were against Georgia at neutral Columbus, at Tallahassee against Florida State, and at Legion Field against the hated down-on-its-luck Crimson Tide. Playing against the best the SEC had to offer, Auburn had scored 132 points and given up only 21 (14 of those in blowouts). Their nearest competitor for the national title was beefy Ohio State of the Big Ten, whose blustery coach, Woody Hayes, infuriated the Auburn faithful by asking, "But *whom* have they [Auburn] played?"

Bill Beckwith was the Auburn sports information director in those days, a stocky young man in horn-rimmed glasses and a flattop crewcut who labored in his disheveled office in the basement of the field house, beyond one end zone of the stadium, where the athletic department was housed in those days. He was shuffling papers, fiddling with statistics, writing press releases, when suddenly he had an epiphany. Any member of the media who subscribed to the Associated Press wire was entitled to vote each week in the AP college football poll. Auburn was within a whisker of the top, thanks to the votes of nearly every major outlet in the South, but Ohio State was atop the rankings due to sheer numbers. It had evolved into regional bias—the South and West against the East and the Midwest—but now Beckwith had made a discovery. The AP rules said *all* media. He made some phone calls and found that about two dozen little radio stations in Alabama alone were not even aware they had a vote. He advised them of that, and then asked them to sit on it: "Don't vote until we've played these next three games."

The players did their part, shutting out Georgia 6–0, lambasting FSU 29–7, and then Beckwith went to work. On the eve of the Alabama game at Legion Field, he and a friendly sports editor and four secretaries got on the horn to scores of small radio stations and newspapers all over the South and issued orders: we're gonna kill Alabama, and as soon as the game ends cast your vote for Auburn. The people at Ohio State never knew what hit them. Shug Jordan pulled his starters early in the second quarter against Alabama, Auburn winning the last showdown before the coming of Paul "Bear" Bryant 40–0, and the dogs were unleashed. The votes for Auburn began rolling in at the Associated Press headquarters at Rockefeller Center in New York, in such an avalanche that the AP sports editor, Ted Smits, phoned Beckwith around dark that evening. "Call 'em off, Bill," he said. "You've won the national championship."

At a ceremony one morning a week or so later, with at least half of Auburn's student body of 8,400 in the stands at little Cliff Hare Stadium, it felt as though Grant was turning over his sword to Lee. Students yelled their *Waaaarr EA-guls* and cheered and cried as Ted Smits handed over a gargantuan silver trophy to Shug Jordan, where he stood in the middle of the field with his players. Auburn, little Auburn, had reached the mountaintop. *Number One.* It was Auburn's first SEC championship team since the conference was organized in 1929, in the midst of the Depression. Shug was selected as the college Coach of the Year by the Quarterback Club in Washington, D. C. Jimmy ("Red") Phillips was a unanimous All-American end. Eight Auburn Tigers were first- or second- or third-team All-SEC. Only four touchdowns were scored on that team, three on passes and one on an interception. Rather than inviting the world to get out of town, Auburn was becoming a member in proud standing.

That was twenty-five years ago, and Auburn hasn't changed much since then. Sure, there are no more dirt paths on campus, and about three per cent of the 18,000 students (up from 8,400) are black, and it is no longer strictly an agricultural-and-engineering school. The old Green House, a crowded buffet-style student eatery, has been replaced by a franchised pizza joint. The athletes live today not in Graves Center but in a dorm that looks like a Holiday Inn. There is a big new coliseum for basketball, and both the stadium and the baseball park have lights. But the Casino and the War Eagle theater and the women's dorms and the frat houses and the belfry of Samford Hall are intact; the KAs still dress like Confederate officers and throw parties on the front lawn beneath the cannon and the Rebel flag; sweet-smelling honeys from Dadeville and Andalusia and Montgomery still check in to check out the flesh; they still speak of the Loveliest Village of the Plain and scream *Waaaar EA-gul* with little provocation and anxiously await the next home football game. In many ways, the more things change the more they remain the same.

The boys of '57 get together now and then, especially on football weekends. They are roughly forty-five years old now and, to a surprising degree, sickness and accidents and bad luck aside, they have led successful and productive lives. Jerry Wilson sells cement in Birmingham. James Warren is an engineer in Louisiana, Zeke Smith works for a pipe company in Birmingham, Jackie Burkett is a pipe-company executive on the west coast of Florida, and Tim Baker—the right guard and captain of that team—is a contractor in Decatur, Alabama, where Lloyd Nix is a dentist. Bobby Hoppe, the bad boy, nearly died of a heart attack, got "born again," and won a humanitarian award while coaching and working with high school kids in central Georgia. Red Phillips, the All-America end, sells State Farm insurance in his hometown of Alexander City. Hindman Wall is the athletic director at Tulane, Ben Preston sells whiskey in Columbus, Georgia, and Morris Savage is a lawyer back home in Jasper. Tommy Lorino, the jet-speed halfback who set an NCAA record by averaging 8.4 yards per carry during that championship season, played in the Canadian Football League, tried running a bar in Birmingham, and wound up working for Xerox in Baton Rouge. Jeff Weakley, a tough undersized guard from Columbus, has fought off cancer. Bobby Lauder, a sub running back, was killed in an automobile accident. And in July of 1980, Shug Jordan died of cancer. Many of his boys showed up for the "private" ceremony in a little church. So did Paul Bryant.

Bear Bryant. That's the name that hangs in the craw of War Eagles to this day. The Alabama-Auburn series began in 1893 with a 32–22 Auburn win. It abruptly ended in 1907 with a 6–6 tie over some vague contractual dispute, and it didn't resume until 1948, when the two schools got together and Alabama won by a score of 55–0. (Auburn fans still plead *"fifty-six! fifty-six!"* from their side of Legion Field whenever it appears Auburn has the upper hand.) The pendulum took a violent swing in Alabama's direction the moment Bryant arrived, his 1958 team (minus some of the best athletes from the 40–0 losers of the year before, due to a Bryant housecleaning) lost by only 14–8, and then it became all-'Bama for a while. The Tide threw shutouts at Auburn in the next four games, began winning national championships of its own, introduced such quarterbacks as Joe Namath and Ken ("Snake") Stabler, and generally hogged the national spotlight even during times when Auburn was doing fairly well in its own right. It rankled.

They were holding their first official reunion twenty-five years later on the first day of May, 1982, the day of the annual A-Day Game that caps spring football practice, to be played that evening at six o'clock in the newly renamed Jordan-Hare Stadium. Auburn was shooting for the unofficial record in attendance for such an affair (they fell just short of Notre Dame's estimated thirty thousand). The A-Day Game is mainly a chance to catch up on fellow alumni and to check out the boys who will make up the team in the coming fall. Almost everybody would be making a trial run for the season. They already had their tickets, had visited Johnston-Malone to buy more Auburn baubles, had even staked out a place to park their campers during each home game. Their gaudy National Championship rings grown as smooth and bald as their heads, wives or second wives at their sides, they were gathered around the pool of a motel on the edge of town at mid-afternoon, in reunion mode: hugs and handshakes, an open bar, tables laden with barbecue and potato salad and beans. "Understand Lorino's down in Mobile now," somebody would say, noticing his absence. "Anybody heard from Jimmy Reynolds lately?" another would ask. And, "Hey, ol' Ronnie Robbs lives somewhere in Tennessee, but he's got an unlisted number." There was much talk of Shug Jordan and the other coaches.

At the motel pool, looking remarkably fit after all of these years, Zeke Smith reflected on the '57 season. In many ways he was the archetypal Auburn player of that time: a drawling country boy, brawny and hungry, out of a high school in the Florida Panhandle so small that it played seven-man football. He and Jackie Burkett had become All-Americans in 1958 and gone on to play in the National Football League. "I can't say I was ever *scared*," he was saying. "I mean, hell, where I came from we didn't have but thirteen players on the team. If I was ever scared, it was when I checked in at Auburn and saw that big stadium and those fancy uniforms." Like many of the others, he was still amazed that the '57 season turned out as it did. "I was wondering that day when Coach Jordan told us about Cook and May how the hell we were going to win a single game. I guess it finally dawned on me that we might make it when we came in at halftime of the Mississippi State game, behind for the first time, and the coaches said don't worry, we're better than anybody, we'll win, and we came back and scored. Then I *knew*."

Pat Meagher ("Marr"), a halfback in '57 who now pilots for American Airlines and lives in Murfreesboro, Tennessee, near Nashville, sat with his family at a Formica-top table and remembered his special moment. He hadn't been a star, but in a freakish way he played a big part that year. On the eve of the third game, after the win at Tennessee and the blowout of Chattanooga, a large crowd of students had assembled at the old wooden barnlike Sports Arena for a Beat Kentucky pep rally. Kentucky was going to be a formidable test, if for no reason other than the presence of a hulking linebacker named Lou Michaels, a violent son of the coal mines, a one-man team who could kick field goals and do everything else. Beat Michaels, you beat Kentucky. Meagher, as president of the A-Club, was summoned to address the pep rally. "We had plenty of confidence by then, had gotten over the loss of Cook and May, were all fired up, but I don't know what got into me. I told that bunch, 'They've got this animal they throw meat to, let him out of the cage once a day'—they went crazy when they heard that—'but I don't care about Lou Michaels. We're better than he is. We're better than *everybody*. We're gonna go *all the way!*' They nearly tore the roof off the Sports Arena when they heard that."

All of this had been sort of a homecoming reunion for me, as well. I had been one of Hoot Gibson's "chow-hall boys" for a couple of years leading up to the 1957 championship season, living in the Graves Center cabins and dishing out three meals a day to the Auburn athletes—earning my room and board by toiling at the chow hall, pitching batting practice for the baseball team at home and on the road, running errands for Bill Beckwith's sports information office—and these men were the closest thing I had to fraternity brothers. As it happened, I gave all of that up when I learned, in the spring of '57, that I would become sports editor of the school newspaper, the *Plainsman,* come fall. It wasn't until the late '90s that it dawned on me that I, too, had benefited from the national title. Going into that season I had been a shy young man, feeling my way into sportswriting at the state's lesser university; coming out of it, having experienced the giddiness of being associated with the best college football team in the United States of America, I found confidence in myself for the first time. *Hey,* I remember thinking, *we're as good as anybody.* It worked that way for all of us, in fact, from the players and coaches to little ol' Auburn itself. When I graduated, I bought one of the last rings that would read Alabama Polytechnic Institute. From then on, it became Auburn University.

Atlanta, 1982

PART THREE The Gloaming

Mister Cobb

THE OZARK BASEBALL CAMP was tucked in a fertile green valley of the low, rolling Ozark Mountains of southeastern Missouri, hard by a state park noted for the trout that could be taken
on fly rods from the spring-fed Current River, a summer play-
ground for boys who dreamed of becoming major-league baseball players. The place was run by a fellow named Carl Bolin, a
former minor-leaguer and high school coach, who raised crops
and livestock "and ballplayers," as he liked to put it, on the land
where he had grown up. Every summer, for three-week sessions
that cost $105 for room and board and "tuition," eighty-five kids
at a time, most of them between the ages of ten and eighteen,
cavorted all day on the two diamonds carved out of Bolin's valley,
being drilled in the fundamentals and playing controlled games.

My first trip to the camp came in 1951, when I was fifteen. I
had answered an ad in *The Sporting News*, eschewing high school
ball that spring in order to work and save money toward the cost,
and in late May took a Trailways bus from Birmingham into the
Ozark hills, in time to work Bolin's fields long and hard enough
to pay for the entire summer. It was heaven. We ate, slept, talked,
and played baseball twenty-four hours a day in that valley, under
the tutelage of Bolin (a "bird-dog scout" who always wore a
hand-me-down New York Giants uniform on the fields) and his
assistants, who included a gnarled old catcher named Wally
Schang, one of Babe Ruth's roommates with the Yankees. The
hills rang with the sounds of boys playing baseball. At one point

we all piled into the back of a truck and rode all the way to St. Louis to catch my first major-league game, the woeful Browns against the mighty Yankees, where Satchel Paige got up from his Naugahyde recliner in the bullpen long enough to throw a "hesitation pitch" that Mickey Mantle hit into the street beyond the right-field stands.

There was no doubt that I would return for the next summer, when I was turning sixteen and beginning to fill out a bit, because this time there would be a "special guest instructor": none other than Ty Cobb, "The Georgia Peach," arguably the greatest player in the history of the game. We were too young to know, and the world at large wasn't quite ready to digest at the time, that Cobb was also a paranoid, wall-to-wall sonofabitch: a big-time gambler too rich from Coca-Cola stock for his own good, a gun-toting, hard-drinking, all-but-certified psychotic wife-beater who had once jumped into the stands to beat up a fan who turned out to be paraplegic. All we knew about was Cobb's .367 lifetime batting average and his more than four thousand base hits in twenty-four seasons, and that he took no prisoners while on the basepaths, brandishing his spikes like scalpels.

How Carl Bolin pulled off such a coup, I'll never know, but one day he called all of us together in the large room that doubled as a dining hall and recreation room to prepare us for Cobb's imminent arrival. "He'll be with us for a week," Bolin said, "and I want you boys to remember that he's our guest. We want to make sure he enjoys himself." He looked around the room to be certain he had everyone's attention. "There are some people who say he was a dirty player, that he took it too far, cut people with his spikes, all of that. Mister Cobb is pretty sensitive about that kind of thing. I don't want to hear any such talk while he's here. Let's think *positive* thoughts. Let's try to learn from him."

It's a wonder we got any work done a couple of days later, the day of Cobb's arrival, between our keeping one eye on the ball during our daily rituals and the other peeled on the gravel road leading from the rickety wooden bridge over the Current River that would bring him into our midst. Wally Schang and the two other full-time instructors, a brawny former minor-league power hitter and an ex-pitcher for the St. Louis Browns, had their hands full. Bolin had driven the 170 miles of twisting asphalt roads to fetch Cobb, who had dropped in on a Cardinals game the night before, and now, in the late afternoon, here came his old station wagon, bumping across the bridge on a grueling return trip that had included an unscheduled stop to repair a flat tire. Many of us rushed to line the road, bats and gloves in hand, for a peek. And there he was, the Georgia Peach, coat off but bowtie firmly in place, sternly waving a hand in salute from the back seat of Bolin's dusty carriage like a king.

Rushing off the fields and to the rustic cabins where we stowed our stuff and slept on cots, we showered and dressed and hustled up the hill to the big house for supper and, finally, an introduction to the great man. He ate what we ate, seated at a table with Bolin and with J. G. Taylor Spink, publisher of *The Sporting News*, who doubtless had played some part in bringing him here, and after the meal he was introduced and stood behind a Ping-Pong table to address us. Platitudes followed, about how we could make it to the big leagues if we worked hard enough, about discipline and hard work and taking care of oneself, about the joys of baseball. Then Bolin asked if anyone wanted to ask a question. There was the shuffling of feet, a lot of coughing, nervous glances back and forth, until finally a kid of about ten years blurted out a question that Bolin, deep in his heart, must have been fearing: "Mister Cobb, did you ever hurt anybody when you played?" A hush fell over the room. Bolin was apoplectic, tried to head off trouble, but Cobb cut him short. "You're damned right I did, son, and I'd do it again." Over the next ten minutes he proceeded to name names, cite offenses, report the consequences—"The sonofabitch threw at me and he got what he had coming," and "Baseball is war, boys," and "I'd kill anybody that got in my way," and so on and so forth, until he was red in the face—and we all had a fine time that night in the cabins, as the cicadas sang and the moon fell over the hills, much better than telling ghost stories.

• • •

Cobb was sixty-five by then, had put away his spikes nearly a quarter of a century before, but you wouldn't have known it from the way he carried himself during those sweltering summer days in the Ozarks. Slightly balding, showing little paunch for a man of his age, he moved like a god from field to field, group to group, boy to boy, during a stay that he extended for an extra week when a stretch of rain hit the camp ("I don't want to short-change the boys"). He was waiting for us after breakfast, when the dew or puddles of rain were on the field, and he was with us after supper when Bolin uncrated training films (*How to Bunt, Making the Double Play, The Hit-and-Run*) to show on a screen hung from the rec room ceiling—adding his own commentary, of course. He was clearly loving this, having a captive audience of adoring young men who wouldn't throw at his head or write bad things about him or try to steal his money. Speaking mainly for myself, I think we loved the old man back, in spite of what we had heard about him.

A Southerner myself, and one who had always leaned toward the rowdier aspects of the game, I was dying to have a private moment with Cobb but didn't quite know how to arrange it. He seemed agreeable enough when approached, as long as the question seemed worthwhile, but I was just a skinny little second baseman who simply lacked the courage to go right up to the great man. On the night before what was to be his last day with us, I hardly slept for thinking how I might have a word with him. I remained silent all through the next afternoon, tongue-tied up until the final minutes, until I knew it was now or never. Everybody seemed to be leaving. The sun was sinking fast. Cobb was walking across the infield, nearing the third-base line, heading toward the cool dugout beyond, when I blurted, "Mister Cobb?"

"Yes?" He was wearing an Ozark Baseball Camp T-shirt, khakis, and Hush Puppies, all caked with dust now. He turned to face me. His famous eyes glared. I shirked, thought about running, but didn't. *Sliding. Ask him about sliding.*

"I can't slide on my right side," I said, almost apologetically.

"Southerner, huh?"

This took me aback. "Yes, sir. Alabama."

"Maybe we're born that way."

"Sir?"

"I was the same way, son." I was aware that everybody else on the field had come to a dead stop. "Let me show you how I did it." With that, Cobb trotted backwards to the shortstop position, crouched with his hands on his knees, scuffed his feet like a bull preparing to set sail, glared at the third-base bag, did everything but snort. A gleam in his eyes showed that something had been awakened in the old warrior, the meanest man in captivity, and then he took off like a madman. He went airborne and hit the bag with a mighty *whummpp,* in a cloud of dust, and when it cleared we could see that he had torn it from its mooring.

"You don't actually slide into it, son," he said, standing and dusting himself off. "You *stomp* the sonofabitch." He didn't have to add that sliding is for sissies.

Sports Illustrated, 1984

12

The Billy Ray Hunsinger Show

RADIO WWJD WAS BORN in failure and has stayed that way. The station was founded in 1964 by a gaggle of patriotic and religious zealots who hoped to help Barry Goldwater, the conservative Arizona senator, take the White House out of the hands of those godless forked-tongued Democrats. During that summer and fall, the fare on the little five-thousand-watt station was relentlessly Christian and fire-breathing Republican, a grab bag of evangelists, gospel singers, syndicated conservative pundits like Paul Harvey, canned campaign rhetoric from Goldwater headquarters, even a weekly show hosted by Lester Maddox, the Georgia governor-to-be, best known for chasing black protesters away from his fried-chicken emporium with an axe handle. When Goldwater was roundly defeated that November, those few people who even knew there ever *was* a WWJD, stuck out there as it was on the far right end of the AM dial at 1690 with the Spanish-language stations, assumed the operation would die as abruptly as it had been assembled.

Not so. The original owners bailed out immediately, secure only in the knowledge that they had created a catchy Christian motto with their call letters (WWJD, for "What Would Jesus Do?"), and in the ensuing years the station got passed around like an unwanted orphan. Under a series of backers, who bought it for reasons ranging from simple ego to being a tax write-off, WWJD has changed its format nearly every six months in its hapless attempts to catch the ears of the public—any public. At one time or another, it has featured rock 'n' roll, rhythm 'n' blues, country, all-talk, all-sports, all-Christian, once even making a stab at becoming "the homemaker's friend" with eighteen solid hours of news about cooking, cleaning, entertaining, and parenting, between reruns of such old-timey soap operas as "Fibber McGee and Molly." Alas, nothing has worked.

But where there's a broadcasting license and a place on the dial there is always hope, and that seems to be about the only bright spot for the latest owner, one Broadus Delany Spotswood, Jr. Built like a bowling ball, right up to his shiny bald head, B.D. has been a force in the earth-moving business—*bidness*—since getting in at the beginning of the interstate highway development period in and around Atlanta. He knows nothing about the radio business, being a graduate in civil engineering from Auburn in the '60s, but in his search for some measure of fame he has set his heart on becoming known as a communications mogul. Even he admits he hasn't made much progress toward that end in the six months he has run WWJD—it still serves up a smorgasbord, from dawn to midnight, of high school sports and preachers and all sorts of music, plus any noncontroversial chatter he can get cheap—but he's been thinking lately of going back to all-sports.

This, of course, is where Billy Ray comes in. B.D. has been a devout fan ever since he, a rabid Auburn man, heard the radio broadcast of that game when the Gunslinger nearly upset Alabama, Auburn's hated cross-state rival, that day in Tuscaloosa. He is, in fact, one of those fans who won't go away—a man who has been sending birthday cakes to Billy Ray every year on the anniversary of that great game, the sixteenth day of October, even when the Gun was living and playing in Canada; who has a huge grainy blowup of the Bear angrily slamming his hound's-tooth hat to the ground at Denny Stadium; who once waited at the bar at Manuel's for three hours in hopes of catching his hero coming through the door; whose dream it is to get a tour, guided by Billy Ray himself, of The Gun Room he's read so much about, maybe even be invited to shoot some eight-ball with the Gun on his famous pool table.

Not one to turn aside adulation, Billy Ray nevertheless has

never quite understood B.D. Spotswood's devotion, bordering on madness, and tries to shake him at every opportunity. Now, though, he seems to be stuck with him. B.D. called the house right after the misfortune at WSB, begging Billy Ray to hear him out, making an outrageous offer for him to host a Sunday night sports call-in show on WWJD. "Hey, Gun, you can say anything you want to on my station," he promised. "We believe in free speech around WWJD." Sensing that he was likely to be headed out the door at any moment, given Ginny's reaction to his latest adventure, Billy Ray had no recourse but to accept the man's offer. After all, he had convinced himself, his audience awaits. And bills must be paid.

He's supposed to meet B.D. at the station at eight o'clock Sunday night so they can go over things before his debut, but finding the place might be a problem. WWJD is located where it's always been, on the Bankhead Highway west of downtown Atlanta, old U.S. 78, the road to Birmingham before it was preempted by I-20. "You can't hardly miss it," B.D. said. "Just look for the busted angel and the tower." The directions, Billy Ray is finding out, are easier given than followed.

Chewing on his cigar, leaning forward on the steering wheel of the Chevy wagon, squinting as he drives straight into the setting sun, he sees the sad remains of a white working-class civilization in its fitful decline. Bud's While-U-Wait Mufflers. Pit Stop Grill. Madam Olga's House of Palmistry. Bernice's Hairstyles. Bubba's Beer Shack. Hub Cap Heaven. Doggy-Do-Rite Obedience School. Tire recappers, used-car lots, camper-body emporiums, drive-in hamburger joints, pawn brokers, gun shops, cut-rate gas stations, auto mechanics; they're all here in a woebegone strip connecting the abandoned roadside towns of Austell and Villa Rica. He is thinking about wheeling into Jo-Jo's Suds for a beer and directions when he finally sees it: a bent metal tower rising through the dusk, sort of an Erector Set version of the Eiffel Tower, with the big block letters WWJD hanging to it more or less vertically.

The station is housed in a low-slung cinder-block building, spray-painted in a heavenly pale-blue and cloudy-white, with the wings of angels sprouting from the roof on either side, a touch left over from the station's beginnings as "The Voice of God in Greater Austell." At some point in time the wings either crumbled or were vandalized, for now their tips dangle and shift in the light breeze, held up only by the bent and rusted wires that once held them together. On one side of the station is Miss Piggy's BBQ, housed in a single-wide trailer encased in a pink adobe shell shaped like a pig; on the other is The Still, in another trailer, this one topped by a fanciful plastic moonshine jug ten feet tall held in place by guy wires.

He bumps off the highway and onto the gravel lot fronting the station. Parked at the base of a flagpole that holds the American flag and the stars-and-bars of the Confederacy, each of them faded and streaked by the elements, are a beat-up Ford pickup and a classic white Cadillac, both caked with dust. He rolls into the space between them, reaches into the back seat for his Packers baseball cap, and takes a deep breath. *Another opening, another show.* He has barely hit the gravel with his booted left foot when he hears a man's voice yelp: "There's my man!" Waddling toward him, all pink skin and pearly teeth, in a wrinkled seersucker suit and Panama hat, is B.D. Spotswood himself.

"Mister Spotswood, I presume."

"Aw, hell, Gun, make it 'B.D.' if you don't mind."

"Okay," says Billy Ray. " 'Gun' 'n' 'B.D.' How's that?"

"We gon' be a great pair, you 'n' me."

"We'll see how it goes, pardner."

B.D. has grabbed Billy Ray's hand with both of his and is vigorously shaking it. Trying to divert the man's attention, as much as anything, Billy Ray points with his free hand to the roof of the building and says, "What's the deal with the wings?"

"Aw, the boys that built the place figured they needed something special to make 'em stand out. A whatchamacallit, a logo, if you get my drift. Pretty damned tacky, if you ask me, but I ain't gon' be the one to test the Lord by taking 'em down. What we need's a good lightnin' bolt to finish the work. That might tell us God don't like 'em, neither." B.D. finally gets the message that Billy Ray would like his hand back, lets go, and invites him into the station. "I swear, this is about the second-greatest day of my life," he says, leading the way, reaching up to wrap a pudgy hand around Billy Ray's shoulder. "Me and you, we're about to make some history, Gun." With the porcine B.D. in his ill-fitting seersucker suit and Panama hat, Billy Ray towering a foot taller in his jeans and cowboy boots and Green Bay cap, they resemble the old comic-strip characters Mutt and Jeff.

If it's possible, the inside of the station appears less promising than the outside. The place looks like one of those machine-gun nests the Germans left behind at Omaha Beach following D-Day: a pillbox, a bunker, a drab windowless redoubt where a man might hole up and fight his last battle. Painted a pale schoolhouse green, illuminated by bluish fluorescent tubes that buzz and flicker at will, floored with black-and-white linoleum squares, it makes your heart sink just to walk through the front door and look at it. To the right is a little reception area, nothing but a torn yard-sale sofa and two mismatched chairs gathered around a low table laden with souvenir ashtrays and old magazines and styrofoam cups holding the moldy remains of days-old coffee. Straight ahead is a Coke machine, a water fountain, a tall wire trash bin overflowing with crumpled balls of paper, and a narrow plywood unisex restroom barely larger than a telephone booth. To the left, at the deeper end of the building, where B.D. is now leading Billy Ray, there are two cramped glass cubicles, beyond which there is a plywood partition with a hollow door marked "Private."

The only sound is the muted singing of Hovie Lister and the Statesmen Quartet, this being the Sunday Night Gospel Hour at WWJD. Perched morosely on a stool at the controls in the engineer's booth, elevated slightly higher than the other glass cubicle, is a sullen-looking young man in his early twenties, woefully thin, wearing a ponytail and earrings and wire-frame glasses. He is wearing headphones, nodding his head to the music, chomping away at a barbecue sandwich brought over from Miss Piggy's. B.D. waves at him, gets a nod in return, and leads Billy Ray over for an introduction.

"Gun, this here's Wally Medders. Call him 'Spider' for obvious reasons. Spider, meet Billy Ray Hunsinger."

The young man rises halfway from his stool, wiping his lips and hands with a paper napkin, extends a greasy handshake. "Nice to meet you," he says. "Old jock, right?"

"Spider here's studying to be a pharmacist," says B.D. "Over at Kennesaw College."

"Drug-pusher, right?" says Billy Ray, returning the insult. The boy shrugs, rolls his eyes, sits back down to his dinner.

"Okay." B.D. clears his throat. "Spider's your engineer. Any problems you get, he'll take care of 'em. He's got enough taped commercials and stuff to last from here 'til Labor Day. Need to pee, just give him a signal. Phone lines go cold, he'll cover. You get tired of runimatin' and need some time to —"

"Say what?"

"*Roonimatin*'. You know, thinkin' out loud. That's what the show's all about."

"He means 'ruminating,'" Spider says to Billy Ray.

"What I said. *Runimatin*'. Anyways, come on in the office here, Gun, so we can talk."

Billy Ray has had a couple of weeks now to ponder the meaning of what happened to him that night on WSB-TV, and he's still in what the shrinks call denial. For two years he'd had a gig every Sunday night on WSB, the dominant television station in Atlanta, doing a three-minute commentary inside a show called "The Locker Room" that followed the late news. Basically, he was paid to run at the mouth—*runimate*—on any sports subject of his choosing: inflated baseball salaries, stupid mascots, college recruiting scandals, artificial turf versus natural grass, pregame prayers, women's basketball, and the like. "Just be yourself, Gun," was the station manager's only advice, and that he had done with great gusto. "Baseball hasn't been the same since they quit break-ing their cigars when they slid into third base," he once remarked. "Puck-off time's seven o'clock," he said of a National Hockey League game. He got into some trouble when he pondered whether the Georgia women's basketball team, the Lady Dogs, shouldn't be called the Bitches, but charmed his way out of it. He dearly loved stock-car racing and pro wrestling, ridiculed tennis and golf ("Meanwhile, in Augusta, the trust-fund babies . . ."). He was a handful, but he knew what his bosses knew: that "Billy Ray's Corner" had been primarily responsible for a steady rise in their Sunday night ratings since its inception. Love him or hate him, just don't ignore him. Getting paid to do what he'd been doing for years as the center of attention at the big round table up front at Manuel's was, to him, a dream job if not an out-and-out scam.

He still doesn't know what hit him. So what if he'd spent a little time with his muse, Jim Beam, during the long hot summer's day; that was nothing new. So what if he'd said what he'd heard a hundred times, at Manuel's and the liquor store and on the streets, about the predominantly black Atlanta Falcons football team; it was just a good-natured comment, all in fun. At any rate, summing up that night's commentary with a few words about the Falcons' prospects for the coming season, he had referred to them as the "Fal-*coons*." Hell, all of the old boys he knew said it all the time. Some of his best friends from the pro football days were black, weren't they? And hadn't "Niggers Go Long" actually been in the playbook at Green Bay, at the suggestion of a hot-shot black receiver, eager to fit in, a rookie out of Florida A&M? So what's the fuss?

Even while he was unhooking the microphone clipped to his blue blazer and dismounting from the stool, he heard not the usual whoops and laughter from the cameramen, among his steadfast fans, but, rather, the mad ringing of telephones. He saw the director, up in the glass booth overlooking the studio, slam his clipboard to the floor. As he walked toward the exit, heading toward his office, he saw his buddies on the floor diverting their eyes. There was a present awaiting him a few minutes later when he arrived at his desk after a stop at the john: the near-empty fifth of whiskey, which somebody had fished from the bottom drawer, now resting like a paperweight on a memo from the show's producer. There were two words, hastily scribbled with a red grease pencil. "You're fired."

• • •

Now, two weeks later, he finds himself sitting in a busted web-and-aluminum lawn chair across the desk from B.D. Spotswood, erstwhile radio magnate, as they talk about the new show's format and matters of technology. "If this thing works, Gun, I'll be replacing that danged alunimun chair." *Al-u-ni-mun.* "Yessiree. It's gon' be gen-u-*wine* black leather, from here on out. Anyways, reckon you might have some questions."

"So all I gotta do is just sit and talk for two hours?" Billy Ray says.

"That's it. Up to you if you want to talk about WSB. I never liked the *agorant* bastards, anyways."

"Who do you figure's listening?

"Don't really know, to tell the truth. Over the years, WWJD's changed clothes more'n a stripper. We got coloreds that think it's still James Brown, good old boys searching for Hank Williams, homemakers wanting to learn how to cook asparagus. I'm gon' spring some money for one o' them audience sur-views once you get started."

Billy Ray looks around the sad office, its stained plywood walls decorated, if that's the word, with Auburn mementos and souvenir silver shovels representing groundbreakings; its grimy linoleum floor littered with stacks of newspapers and trade magazines; B.D.'s desk a jumble of tapes and press releases and unopened mail. He winces now to recall the broken angel wings outside on the forlorn Bankhead Highway, a long way from the staid white-columned fortress of WSB on Peachtree Street, and the general seediness he encountered upon entering the building. He leans sideways to knead his jock itch, the curse of his life, then looks B.D. square in the eye. "I don't know about this deal," he says.

B.D. Spotswood won't be denied. "If it's about money . . ."

"Aw, naw. Five hundred bucks a night's about twice what I was getting over there. What I'm wondering is . . . well, hell, it don't seem like your signal would go much beyond metropolitan Austell, if you don't mind my saying."

"Nosir. No . . . *sir!* Got that worked out, first thing. Turned that transpitter around, aimed it on downtown Atlanta like them damned Yankees did their guns, took care of that real quick.

Right about now, when these little ol' pissant day stations go off the air"—looking at his watch, seeing it is nine o'clock already—"hell, we get right into Atlanta like we was a local station. Yessir. We're playing with the big boys now. Look out, Atlanta."

They seem to be grandiose plans, indeed, and Billy Ray knows he is in no position to negotiate. He'll play it as it lays, give it a shot, see how it goes. It beats not working at all, which hasn't helped his spirits of late. Loony as this fellow B.D. seems, not to mention the snarly hippie engineer, Spider, he's being given a blank check, handed the ball, invited to make up the plays as he goes along. It'll be called "Jock Talk with Billy Ray Hunsinger," ten-to-midnight Sundays, open-mike, let 'er rip.

"Lookie here, now, Gun"—B.D. takes another glance at his watch—"hate to miss your very first show, but I gotta run. My mama's waiting up for me, still pissed I didn't make community with her this morning. You know how them Cacklicks are. Gon' cost me supper at a fancy restaurant."

"So it's me and Spider."

"Don't worry. I'll be listening in to see how it goes, but I figure y'all can take care of things."

"Just give the ball to Gun, right?"

"You got it." B.D. frowns, searching his mind. "Oh, yeah," he says. "You might want to steer things around politics and religion, *contraservial* stuff like that. We ain't got one o' them time-delay gizmos yet, so you might oughta cut 'em off if they get to cussin'. Last thing I need's trouble about my license. People want football, Gun"—*FUH-baw*—"so let's give it to 'em, okay?" B.D. suddenly kicks back his chair, shuffles out in front of the desk, goes into a rigid crouch to emulate a quarterback going under center to take the snap. "Hut!-hut!-hut!!!" he shouts. "*FUH-baw*, Gun. *FUH-baw*." And then he's out of there, like a receiver hauling ass on a post pattern.

Billy Ray follows him to the door, watches the Cadillac throw up a roostertail as B.D. hurtles out of the lot onto the Bankhead Highway, choked, even at this hour, with lumbering church buses and frisky pickups and belching eighteen-wheelers. He crunches across the gravel lot to Miss Piggy's BBQ, crowded with teenaged boys ogling pony-tailed girls, buffing the new paint jobs on their hotrods, showing off new tattoos—apparently, it's the place for teenagers to hang out in Austell on a Sunday night—orders a barbecue and fries and a tall Coke with lots of ice, then returns to his faithful wagon, Rosinante, parked below flags now drooping in the hot windless sky. Opening the rear gate, he rummages through a box holding dusty plastic toys that have been there since Maggie was a toddler, fishes out a fresh fifth of Jim Beam, locks up, and trudges back into the station.

He has always felt like an admiral at the bridge of a battleship in these studios, surrounded as he is by a console of luminous dials and toggle switches and mysterious knobs, a silver boom mike on a flexible crane neck, a telephone with a half-dozen pushbuttons that can light up and blink, a set of headphones so you can keep your hands free while conversing. Sunk deep in a cushy executive's swivel chair that enables him to roll free in the slot of a U-shaped counter, punching this button or that one, free to grimace or shoot a bird or make a face at the unseen voice on the other side of the phone, under the benevolent gaze of an engineer in the opposite sound booth, he is the center of attention, the star of the show, the commander-in-chief, the engine that drives the machine. He feels the same God-like power that he did when he was the Gunslinger, under center, checking out the defense, deciding which of his receivers he would bless this time with a bullet on the numbers.

"Ol' B.D.'s something, ain't he?" Billy Ray is saying to Spider.

"He's one for the becord rooks, all right." Spider's demeanor toward Billy Ray has changed dramatically since the moment Gun came back with dinner, uncorked the Jim Beam, and gulped three times straight from the bottle.

"Hope he don't screw up my paycheck like he does the English language."

"You should've been here the night he decided to sing 'The Star-Spangled Banner' to go off the air. *A capella.*"

"You're shitting me. *Nobody* can sing that damned thing."

"I kid you not. Said, 'Now, I'd like to honor our forecestors by singing the "Star-Studded Anthem," archipelago.'"

"*Archipelago?*" Billy Ray, in the midst of taking another swig when Spider recounts the story, spews whiskey all over the console. "How'd he do?"

"Started out fine." Spider sings in falsetto, "'Ooh, saay, can you seeeee . . .' Then he got lost. 'Purple mountains' ma-jes-teeee . . .' Good thing I'd already shut down the phone lines."

They're still yukking it up when Spider checks the clock. Three minutes 'til ten. They've already been over the routine, the phone lines and the cues and the commercial breaks and what little else Billy Ray needs to know, so now he's on his own. Soon Spider is in his booth, counting down the seconds—four, three, two, one—then stabbing his index finger at Billy Ray, mouthing the word "go." Showtime.

Howdy and a good evening to you, sports fans. It's the Gunslinger here, Billy Ray Hunsinger, talking sports with y'all over WWJD in beautiful downtown Austell, Georgia. Ain't nobody here but me and my engineer Spider and my good buddy Jim Beam. We're gonna be here 'til midnight, taking your calls and talking football or whatever comes to mind. All you got to do is give us a call at—where's that number at, Spider?—here we go, write this down. It's Ask Jock, that's A-S-K J-O-C-K, two-seven-five, five-six-two-five. Got that? We'll be right back, folks. Gotta pay some bills . . .

Hell, this deal might just work out. While Spider slaps on some commercial tapes, for dog food and used cars and an outlet store, Billy Ray pours some more bourbon into his tall cup of Coke and ice. The thought is crossing his mind that he might wind up sitting here for the full two hours, talking to himself, when he sees one of the buttons on the phone blinking red. A caller! He can't wait for the commercials to end.

Hey, there, Gun, ol' buddy.
Yo.

I bet you don't know who this is.

What the hell kinda —. Excuse me, folks. Naw, 'fraid you got me there. You're gonna have to give me a clue.

Tuscaloosa. October the sixteenth, nineteen damned sixty-five.

I'm gonna have to ask you to watch your language there, friend. Boss's orders. Plus, I gotta eat.

Sorry, Gun. Anyhoooo. That date ring a bell in that ol' hard head o' yours?

Wait a minute. This ain't, aw, shoot, gimme a second. Is this ol' Peahead? North Alabama State Catamounts, nineteen sixty-five?

The one and only.

Bobby Gillespie. You old dog. Folks, this old boy saved my life that day we almost beat 'Bama and the Bear. He could block an Allied Freight Line truck, fully loaded. Didn't see you at the reunion last spring, Peahead.

Me and the wife was sick, both of us. Heard about your little adventure, though.

Well, that's another story for another time. Not much I can say that wasn't in the Birmingham paper. What're you up to these days, anyhow, buddy?

Sanitation engineer, Gun. Over in Villa Rica.

That's a fancy word for garbage collector, ain't it?

If you want to put it that way.

I'm sorry to hear 'bout that, Peahead.

Aw, it ain't so bad, Gun. Sometimes they let me drive. . . .

This is great! Billy Ray is having the time of his life. He eats up nine minutes with Peahead Gillespie, the center on that great team, just carrying on about the old days and how the others are doing now. Then comes another of his old teammates, Stork Sims, his ace receiver, now a postman, and they cover another eleven minutes discussing how they almost made a believer out of Bear Bryant that day by totalling 521 yards passing. There is even a call from the enemy, a fellow identifying himself as Ben Burns, "Scottie" Burns, who had been in the stands with the Alabama band on that long-ago October afternoon and recalls it as the "highlight of my four years at the Capstone, if you throw out the drinking." He plays it straight when there is another call, this from B.D. Spotswood, thinly disguising his voice and identifying himself only as "an Auburn fan" wanting to know how it looks this year for the Tigers, saying how much he loves the show, especially his "runimations" on the game.

When they reach the end of the first hour, that's it, only those four calls, and that's fine by Billy Ray. He'd just as well rock back and forth in the swivel chair, sip whiskey, tell his stories, make monkey faces at Spider through their respective studio windows, rather than be interrupted by God-knows-who on the phone lines. At eleven o'clock, time for Spider to plug in to the network for ten minutes of news, sports, and weather, then to strip and read some copy off the Georgia Network News wire, Billy Ray takes the bottle outside for some fresh air. Except for an occasional police cruiser and a Greyhound and a Peterbilt trudging along under the sliver of a new moon, the Bankhead Highway is virtually empty now, reminding him of winter in the Canadian Rockies.

So far, so good, he's thinking. Piece of cake. Settling into his chair after the break, forty-five minutes to go, feeling good, deciding to talk a little about the flap at WSB, he signs on again. "Give us a call at A-S-K J-O-C-K, that's two-seven-five, five-six-two-five," he says, hoping nobody will. He's doing a dance step around the issue, explaining as how he didn't mean anything personal by saying "Fal-*coons*," and going into some detail about how it was a black player, after all, who had come up with the description "Niggers Go Long" for one of their favorite pass routes during his days with the Green Bay Packers, when the red pushbuttons on his phone begin blinking like Christmas-tree lights.

Line One. You're on the air.

So there you are. Thought you'd been lynched, bubba.

Who'm I talking to?

What do you care? I'm just another nigger to you.

Hold on there, just hold on. We can't be using that kind of language here.

You honkie motherfucker—

That's it, pal. Line Two. The Gun speaking. Who we got?

You don't know yo' ass from a goalpost, you —

Lookie here, sports fans, I've told you about the cussing. Let's everybody calm down, now, just calm down. Line Three, we're talking football.

Brother Hunsinger?

This is Billy Ray Hunsinger.

It's a pleasure to speak to you, sir.

Who've we got here?

This is the Reverend T. Vivian Beaumont of the First Calvary AME Revival Assembly on Moreland Avenue.

Yes, sir, preacher. Got the football fever, do you? Won't be long now, you know, before the boys start bustin' heads.

Well, sir, first of all I want to apologize for some of the brothers. I'm sure they know better than to use that kind of language.

Thanks, Rev. That okay, to call you Rev?

Long as I might refer to you as Brother Gun.

I been called worse.

As have I, sir.

So what's on your mind, Rev?

Well, sir, I've got a little riddle for you.

This is different. Go ahead, Rev, what you got?

I was wondering if you know the difference between the N-C-A-A and the N-A-A-C-P.

Sure, I do, Rev, and I've got a good story about that.

I'm sure you do. You're a wonderful storyteller. But I've come to you this evening—

Back in the '50s when Auburn kept getting in trouble with the N-C-A-A for buying players, they had this colored boy who was kinda like a mascot. LEE-roy. Must've been eighty years old. Anyway, he goes up to Shug Jordan one day when they'd just learned Auburn had gotten another two years of no bowl games, and he says, Coach, I just can't figure out this En Double-A Cee Pee. First, they're wantin' to make us to go to school with white folks, next thing you know they're puttin' us on prohibition.

I fail to see the humor in that, Brother Gun.

Naw, see, he just couldn't get 'em straight. The En-Cees and the Double-As, and then that Pee thrown in.

What you fail to understand, sir, is that these are racist comments. For one thing, how can you refer to an eighty-year-old man as a boy?

Oh, come on, Rev—

That is most demeaning, sir, to a very large segment of our population.

I don't see why you people—

That, too, Brother Gun. "You people." Who are "you people"?

Well, you know. Y'all. Black folks. But, hey, I don't mean anything by that. They're just words. You know what they say. Sticks and stones might break my bones, but words ain't never gonna bother me.

You're good, Brother Gun. Now I've forgotten my riddle.

I think it was, What's the difference between the NCAA and the NAACP?

That's right. Do you know the answer?

Well, let's see. You've got the National Collegiate Athletic Association, and the National Association for the Advancement of Colored People. Hunh. I don't know. You got me.

There's not a bit of difference in them, Brother Gun.

I don't follow you, Rev.

They're both for helping the less fortunate to realize their dreams.

Whoa, wait up a minute, Rev. That's a bit of a stretch, don't you think? One of 'em's about football, and the other one's about, you know, something else.

No, sir, not quite. They both stand for the same thing: opportunity. Now that the NAACP's done its job, don't you see, the NCAA can get on with its job. What I'm saying is, no matter the race or creed or color, the Lord loves 'em, like Coach Jake Gaither used to say down at Florida A&M: agile, mobile, and hostile. Understand what I'm saying?

I heard that one, but —. Hunh?

And about that sticks and stones business. Looks to me like you would've learned by now that words can harm you.

But I've tried to explain all of that.

I know, Brother Gun, and I commend you for that. It's gon' be nice, working with you.

Hey, wait just a minute here, Rev.

You have a good evening, now, sir.

Angry callers are lighting up the switchboard again, some laughing and others wanting a piece of either Billy Ray or the preacher, all of them spouting blue streaks of profanity, demanding to be heard. With a full twenty minutes to go, Spider simply shuts down the phone lines, scrawling a note and waving it at Billy Ray—TECHNICAL DIFFICULTIES!!!—who fans himself, greatly relieved, and rambles on about the particular difficulties of playing in snowstorms in the Canadian Football League until he runs out of steam and finally collapses across the finish line.

At midnight, following the last strains of the national anthem, he and Spider are finishing off the fifth of Jim Beam while sprawled over the torn sofa near the front door of the studio. The phones are still ringing, but they can forget that now. Other than their voices, the only other sounds come from faulty plumbing and the flickering fluorescent tubes.

"God *damn,*" says Billy Ray.

"Man, B.D. better get that time-delay fast, before the FCC gets here."

"I thought you were gonna be screening the fuckers."

"These guys were too quick for me, Gun."

"You mean you couldn't just *feel* it coming? Guy comes on and the first thing he says is 'honkie motherfucker'?"

"Hey," Spider says, "they all sounded like preachers when I talked to 'em. The 'motherfucker' guy told me he was a huge fan of yours. Talked real calm and respectable. Wadn't much I could do—."

Suddenly the door flies open, freezing Spider in mid-sentence. It is B.D., in his Teddy-bear pajamas and a purple velour robe, sweating and flailing his arms and sputtering, Elmer Fudd on a rant. "*FUH-baw,* Gun, I said *FUH-baw,* hot dammit! How'm I gon' get to be a radio magnet if you ain't talkin' *FUH-baw*? Hanh? I'm bumfuzzled, boys, utterly complexed. Spider, I'll deal with you later. Gun, me 'n' you got some serious runimatin' to do."

From *Nobody's Hero*, 2002

13

On the Bus

AT MIDNIGHT THE BULB-NOSED bus creaked eastward across the wasted Florida Panhandle, wheezing along U.S. 90 past darkened farmhouses and deserted towns and Burma Shave signs and scrubby pastures. The bus had been given up for dead five years earlier by the Jackson County Board of Education, passed on to the Singing Tillman Family, and finally turned over to the Graceville Oilers Boosters Club Inc. when Orville Tillman ran off with a church secretary. The Boosters had sprayed the bus royal blue and hand-lettered in white the legend GRACEVILLE OILERS ALA-FLA LEAGUE on both sides and across the back, and in the four years it had been used to transport the club to the other points in the league—Dothan, Crestview, Fort Walton Beach, Panama City, Eufaula, Opp, Andalusia—it had been held together by a succession of relief pitchers who knew more about replacing ruptured oil pans than getting batters out. Now the seats danced from their moorings, the door did not always open, the reverse gear was a memory, the blue paint was fading to turquoise, and most of the windows had been smashed since the night an indiscreet rookie left-hander named Bubba Byrd threw his high hard one at the head of the Fort Walton Beach Jets' hero during a road game. In a moment of inspired exasperation the players had dubbed her the Blue Bitch.

They had lost again, this time to the Crestview Indians by a score of 14–2, their cause affected not a little by eight errors, and after the game they had quickly showered and dressed and then crept in silence to a truck stop near De Funiak Springs where they slumped over hamburgers and French fries and Jax beer. Now the bus was crossing the Choctawhatchee River near Westville and Caryville, a full moon following them as they lurched along the highway, still nearly an hour to go on the seventy-eight-mile journey back to Graceville. Paco Izquierdo, a toothy little Mexican who played shortstop and picked up an extra seventy-six dollars a month driving the bus, rode high like a jockey in the driver's seat, muttering in Spanish and squinting through the bug-spattered windshield at the lights of the big diesels chugging toward him. Most of the others were gamely trying to sleep in the suffocating night air, their lank arms and legs sprawling over the ripped seats and spilling into the aisle, a clutter of sweaty bodies whence came a disjointed cacophony of snores, burps, yawns, and farts. The veterans, Buster Smeraglia and Corky Lucadello, a pair of damaged men who had played out this scene for a composite total of forty-two years, had long ago learned how to sleep through anything. It was different with the young players—seventeen-year-old Scooter Cagle was popping pimples and staring emptily at the moon; Knucks Chappell, the nineteen-year-old knuckleball pitcher, was aimlessly filing his long fingernails; and bug-eyed Whiz Whisenant was holding a towelful of ice to his head to ease the pain from a crash into the outfield wall—for it wasn't easy to go from Mama's cooking to Class D baseball overnight.

Stud Cantrell, the Oilers' player-manager, had commandeered the wide seat at the rear for himself and the girl. Together they had almost killed the fifth of Old Crow, and he was sure she had passed out. Giving up at trying to shift her leaden body into a more comfortable position against the window, he lay back and threw his booted feet on the back of the seats in front of him and tilted his white cowboy hat forward and continued plumbing his repertoire of country songs—

When a woman gets the blues
She hangs her little head and cries

But when a man gets blue
He grabs him a train and rides. . . .

—and tried to remember her name. She was about eighteen, blonde, probably just out of high school. He had seen her hanging around before the game, in short-shorts and a narrow halter showing huge breasts, and he could tell that she was ready the way a farmer knows when a heifer is ready. When the score had reached 10–1 in the fifth inning, he managed to get himself thrown out of the game, winked at her as he strode to the clubhouse under a barrage of rolled-up Dixie cups, jumped into his clothes without showering, met her at the bus parked under the pines beyond the right field fence, locked the door, draped his sopping uniform shirt over the rear window, and screwed her on the back seat. He plied her with the Old Crow on the way out of Crestview, mounting her again while his players were inside eating at the truck stop, and he was reasonably confident of yet another encore once he got her back to his room in the more alluring surroundings of the Panhandle Hotel in Graceville.

One of these mornings
I'm sure gonna leave this town
'Cause a trifling woman
Sure keeps a good man down. . . .

"Can't you cut that shit out?" Eyes half open, pulling a blue warmup jacket tight around her arms, she curled her legs under her body and tried to find a soft place on the muddy chest protector she had rolled up to use as a pillow.

"Thought you'd passed out on me," he said.

"With that racket?"

"Racket? That's the king of country music."

"Screw him."

"Can't. Died more'n ten years ago."

"Too fucking bad. Where are we at, anyway?"

"Florida. Sunshine State. You know, you sure got a bad mouth for a little girl. If some of my fans was to hear a lady friend of mine talk like that, they'd disown me."

"*Where* in Florida? When the hell are we going to get off this bus? My goddam back's killing me."

"Ain't but one way to find out," he said, uncapping the bottle and draining it until there was only an inch left in the bottom. "And that's to go right up and ask our friendly, courteous driver. If Paco don't know, we're in trouble. Want a sip?" She shook her head furiously and slumped down into the corner again, sullen and drunk. He was sure she had gone under this time. With a shrug he finished off the bottle, sailed it through one of the broken windows, fished the harmonica from his jeans, stretched himself out again, and worked on "Orange Blossom Special."

As the bus droned on through the darkness, the slapping of the tires on the swollen joints of the road keeping time with the music, he felt it coming back to him. These were the worst times, late at night, when the utter finality of his descent was so painfully clear: game over, lights out, booze gone, woman asleep. He had not experienced eight straight hours of sleep since the day he turned thirty and realized his bubble had burst. "Yeah," he was fond of saying, "I got a great future behind me."

Now Stud Cantrell was scraping the bottom. He was thirty-nine, his eyes were not as trusty as they once were, his bad leg ached constantly, and he was haunted by devils when he tried to sleep. He had been fired for failing to win a pennant at Quitman, in the Georgia State League, the year before, and was close to giving up baseball—for what, he had no earthly idea—when he received a last-minute call from Graceville. It was the smallest town in organized baseball and it was not Stud Cantrell's kind of town: few loose women, seedy bars, only one pool hall. The Alabama-Florida League, too, was very possibly the worst Class D League remaining. Only Dothan had a full working agreement, with the St. Louis Cardinals, and all the other clubs were stocked with skittery unwanted rookies earning $150 a month and a scattering of scaly old pros who were, like Stud, waiting for the other shoe to drop. Stud found himself managing the club, playing first base, pitching when nobody else was up to it, watering the infield grass, driving the bus in relief of Paco Izquierdo, searching for ballplayers, nursemaiding the rookies, talking the other veterans out of quitting, throwing batting practice, hitting infield, and keeping up with the equipment. For this he was paid $475 a month, plus his rent at the Panhandle, plus the customary $1.25-a-day meal money, usually for hamburgers, when there was a game on the road.

The Blue Bitch, the town, the pathetic little ballpark, the ragged uniforms, the pay, the opposition—none of it rhymed with what Cecil Cantrell had in mind when, twenty years earlier, he had left the tobacco lands of North Carolina to seek his fortune in the Great American Game.

Drained of energy by the game and the blonde and the booze and the bus, Stud dropped his feet to the floor and eased up in the seat. The girl was embalmed now. His knee had stiffened in the cool air whistling through the windows, and he winced as he stood up. Holding on to the backs of the seats, stepping over the tangle of legs littering the aisle, feeling the effects of the Old Crow, he worked his way to the front of the bus and plopped into the seat across from Paco Izquierdo.

"Got the Rose of Crestview back there, Paco."

"*Si?*" Paco grinned, comprehending nothing.

"Got *mucha muchacha* back there. *Buena* pussy."

Paco's face lit up. "Pussy. *Si. Muy Buena.*"

"Miss Crestview don't think much of your bus, though."

"*Si. Mees* Crestview. *Buena* pussy."

"You poor bastard. Where the hell we at?"

"*Que?*"

"Where the hell's Graceville? Jesus, I got a goddam wetback hitting .150 and he can't even read the trademark on his bat. *Donde esta la* fucking Graceville?"

Paco grinned again and pointing to a sign coming up, a gaudy hand-painted billboard advertising WGOD radio and showing a smiling picture of Oilers owner Talmadge Ramey, and Paco said, "*Aqui.*" Stud gave the finger to the billboard and said, "Stop at the hotel first."

Paco had learned long ago the importance of acting dumb. So he pretended not to know English. "*No comprendo,*" he said.

"El hotel. Primero."

"Si, el hotel. Comprendo. Bueno."

"You hang in there, Paco," Stud said, getting up and swaying toward the rear of the bus. "Only words you gotta know in this league are 'I got it,' 'hamburger,' and 'pussy.'"

"Si, pussy. *Muy buena."*

"Them and 'niggers,'" Stud mumbled, subsiding onto the rear seat.

The town, illuminated by a scattering of streetlights, was closed up tight. Two stray male dogs had squared off in front of Cash Drugs, preparing to do combat over a female hovering in the shadows. The smell of rain was being brought in on the wind, which sent small twisters of dust whirling crazily across Brown Street. When the bus shuddered to a stop in front of the Panhandle Hotel, some of the players began to stir and moan. Paco jerked the door handle, but it wouldn't work, and he cursed in Spanish. Standing on the bottom step, Stud gave the door a violent kick with the sole of his boot, and the door banged open. "You got trouble when you gotta import 'em," he said, staggering across the sidewalk under the dead weight of Miss Crestview, slung over his shoulder like a sack of flour.

From *Long Gone,* 1979

14

Whatever Happened to What's-His-Name?

IT PROMISED TO BE ANOTHER one of those days on that softly undulating farmland where Oklahoma, Kansas, and Missouri run together. By three o'clock in the afternoon the temperature was moving on a hundred, and there was a particular suffocating stillness in the air. Grasshoppers hustled inside every time a screen door opened. Newspapers in the scattered towns and villages warned against the watering of lawns, lest there be no water by August. Trying to ward off the heat, Bruce Swango loosened his tight orange Banlon at the neck and stuck his head out the window so the wind created by the speed of his pale green camper would whistle through his crewcut. When you are born in a land like this, you learn to cope. "Thought I'd stop by at the folks' place for a minute," Swango said, jamming a Roi-Tan Blunt deeper into one corner of his mouth. He is 35 now and has seen a lot of America since he got $36,000 from the Baltimore Orioles and went off to find fame and fortune seventeen years ago. But he remains pure Okie, with a massive upper torso and a red face and barn-door ears and a way of making the words "hired" and "tired" come out *hard* and *tard*.

"They used to write how a scout seen me warm up in the barn, but I think it was some of them New York writers that never seen the barn," he said, bouncing onto a dusty gravel road leading up to the white frame farmhouse where he was born and raised, on a 240-acre spread outside the community of Welch, Oklahoma (pop. 500). "Right here's where me and my brother used to play ball. It was a home run if you hit the ball from the barn to the water pump."

"It's a long way from here to Baltimore," I said.

"Yeah, well, that was part of my problem."

"I talked to Richards the other day."

The mention of Paul Richards, the former Baltimore general manager, stunned him. "What'd Paul say?"

"Didn't want to talk about it."

"That figures."

Finding both of his parents gone, Swango stood in the center of the darkened living room staring at the clutter of old family portraits and photographs. "Reckon why Paul did what he did?" he said, as though talking to himself. "I wasn't no big-league pitcher. Heck, no, they wouldn't a-let me go if I was a big-league pitcher. It's just the way they done it. See, when Baltimore signed me that made it five bonus boys they had to keep on their bench. There was this rule. You get to keep $4,000, right away you got to stay on the big-league roster two years. Well, you can't win no pennant like that. So what Richards wanted to do, he wanted to release me and then sign me back again a year later. When he released me he said, 'Don't pay any attention to anything you read in the paper.' Well, the next day when I got home I read that Swango was too wild and couldn't pitch in front of crowds. I don't know whether Paul told 'em that or not, but somebody sure did. That's what disgusts me. There wasn't none of it true. They was just trying to scare off the other scouts. But two months ago, right here in my home town, they had an Associated Press story in the paper saying how much crowds frustrated me and Baltimore released me and nobody ever heard of me again. Seventeen years later I'm still trying to live it down."

"At least you got some money," I said.

"Did that, all right."

"What'd you do with it?"

"Built a house, bought some cattle."

"You seem to regret the whole thing."

"Naw," he said, closing the door to the house and walking back to the camper. "Not really. You can't turn down that kind of money. I think I had big-league ability, but I needed experience. If you were a bonus ballplayer you didn't have the chance to go out to the minors and learn how to pitch. I do wish I'd a-kept on playing instead of quitting like I did. I think I could have made it back up to the big leagues. Oh, well," he said, cranking the engine, "working the graveyard shift in a *tahr* plant may not sound like much, but it pays good and I get to hunt and fish a lot." With a Babe Ruth League game to coach in a couple of hours, Swango slithered down the gravel road. "Had a big traffic jam on this old road when I was a boy," he said. "One day we counted nine cars parked out here, a big-league scout in every one, all of 'em waiting his turn to go in the house and talk me into signing."

Now, almost two decades later, Bruce Swango and scores of others seem like antiques: names and faces, vaguely recalled, from another era. Teenagers transformed into legends before they were old enough to shave, they live today with the memories of shattered expectations and broken dreams. They were the original "bonus babies" of baseball, as they came to be called, precocious young athletes who were given anywhere from $35,000 to $100,000 as bonuses to sign contracts with major-league clubs suddenly gone bananas over the improbable idea of buying themselves instant pennants or, at the very least, instant superstars.

It was a time unlike any other in American sport. Football and basketball bonus babies of later years were college men, older and comparatively more sophisticated, already tested by top competition. The baseball phenoms were uneducated high school kids, their experience often limited to American Legion games in ball parks where cows grazed behind the outfield fence. They were pursued not by one team from each of two competing pro leagues but by every team in major-league baseball. Although there were some bonus players before and after, the period ran roughly from 1947 to 1955. During that span some one hundred players received a total of more than $6 million in bonuses. In general, the players' individual overnight affluence was the only positive result. Nobody ever won a pennant with bonus players.

Baseball almost went broke. Fans lost respect for owners. Veteran stars protested the reckless spending, bringing some clubs to the brink of mutiny. Most of the young players, pressured to produce, had their careers stunted from the start.

Exactly how it all began, no one seems to know, but once bonus fever set in there was no stopping it. The first pure bonus baby was Dick Wakefield, who had a couple of good wartime seasons with the Detroit Tigers after signing in 1941 but folded when the men came back home. The true beginning of the era came in the late 1940s when the Braves gave $65,000 to an eighteen-year-old left-hander named Johnny Antonelli and the Phillies shelled out some $145,000 for pitchers Robin Roberts, Curt Simmons, and a Georgia country boy named Hugh Frank Radcliffe. When all except Radcliffe showed immediate promise in the major leagues, everybody went crazy.

It was a zany, hysterical, frantic time. The day after high school graduation, strapping young prospects embarked on a summer tour of major-league ballparks, where they would pitch or take batting practice for the brass before finally—around World Series time, when there had been enough time for the bidding to get completely out of hand—signing for something like $75,000. The scouts out in the boondocks, well aware that they could be stamped as lifelong geniuses by finding just one kid who made it, lost their perspective: laying intricate smokescreens for their peers, beating the bushes, finding "another Bob Feller" on every farm, turning in embellished reports on kids who didn't even own a pair of baseball shoes. The owners, too, became addicted: they signed one bonus baby, then had to have another and then another. To the initial delight of the baseball hierarchy—which enjoyed being portrayed as spending enormous sums to bring its fans a winner—the press regularly exaggerated the size of bonus payments and created dozens of premature folk heroes out of kids who had never batted against a curve ball. Despite the exaggerations, the spending was prolific. By the early 1950s the owners were moved to legislate against their own greed and recklessness. Any player signing for more than $4,000 had to take a place on the big-league roster for two years before he could be shipped to the minors. Typically, the "bonus rule" had only negative results. The huge payments continued unabated—though sometimes under the table—but the young prospects' chances for success were drastically reduced. Forced to sit in big-league dugouts—gaining no experience, ostracized by jealous teammates, eventually a source of humor for fans and press—they waited while their potential, assuming they ever had any, stagnated and often disappeared. Many youngsters became convenient scapegoats for scouts and executives who publicly ridiculed them (even inventing fictitious explanations for the players' failure) to cover up for their own poor judgment.

Of the hundred or so bonus babies of that era, no more than a dozen made it in style: Al Kaline, Sandy Koufax, Harvey Kuenn, Roberts, Simmons, et al. They are far outweighed by the ones like pitcher Billy Joe Davidson, who got $60,000 from the Indians in 1951 when he was 17 years old, hurt his arm, never pitched a major-league inning and at 25 was back home in North Carolina pitching to his father in the backyard. In 1955 the Orioles had more than $200,000 tied up in five bonus players they had to keep in Baltimore, and the results were catastrophic: Swango never pitched a big-league game and the other four had a composite Baltimore production of five home runs, forty-nine runs batted in and a .190 batting average. "I swore then," says Paul Richards, "that I'd never sign a kid without seeing him with my own eyes." For most of the bonus babies it was a matter of taking the money and running, usually back to the minor leagues for a while, where they labored as curios until they had proven to themselves that they would never go back up, finally dropping out and going back home to dull jobs and yellowed press clippings and childhood sweethearts. And memories.

"Nothing like a danged old tight T-shirt to let everybody know how fat you're getting." Bruce Swango had poured himself an iced tea glass full of Canadian whiskey and water before going back to the bedroom to change, and now he was padding into the living room in the uniform of the "Rebels," the local Babe Ruth League team. The Swangos and their two young children live in a

Permastone-front house, close to town and the B.F. Goodrich tire plant, where Bruce is "just an ordinary laborer" from midnight to eight in the morning. He owns two lots at the end of the block so he can keep his four bird dogs penned up. "I must be twenty pounds overweight," he said.

Swango's wife, Joann, is a petite blonde from nearby Commerce, Mickey Mantle's hometown. She met Bruce the summer he came home from Baltimore, and married him a year later. Possessed with that fierce frontier resiliency of Oklahoma women, she was calmly laying out a huge, rushed-up country dinner of roast beef and vegetables so Bruce and fourteen-year-old Scott, who plays second base for the Rebels, could make it to the ballpark on time. Cara Jo, their nine-year-old daughter, was at the moment playing a softball game. "Yeah," said Bruce as everybody sat around the table, "if ol' Scott had his desire and Cara Jo's talent, he'd be something else."

Swango swallowed a roll. "I've tried not to push him, though," he said. "I've seen too many boys who wanted to play real bad and just didn't have the talent. Heck, I was like that. You can fool around too long at something you aren't good at, and it'll mess you up. Scott, now, he's real good with the saxophone. Been talking about giving it up because it's 'sissy,' but I tell him he better keep on playing that saxophone." After a second helping he shoved away from the table. "Be ready soon as I get my spikes," he said. He had an afterthought: "Guess what? They're the same spikes I *retahrd* in."

Of all the stories about the bonus babies, the most bizarre—and yet, because it contains so many universalities, the most nearly typical—is that of Bruce Swango. He grew up working in his father's fields and walking back and forth a mile each way to a country school that had thirteen kids in its eight grades, and never played any organized sports until he enrolled in the tiny high school at Welch. One spring his coach told him if he would try pitching he might be able to get a college baseball scholarship. "That taught me a notion," says Swango.

In his first game as a pitcher he beat archrival Miami, 1–0, with 13 strikeouts. He was a bit wild, but what farm boy with a blazing fastball isn't? He continued to pitch, for the strong Tri-State Miners and other semipro teams in the area. This is baseball country, where such major leaguers as Mantle, the Boyer brothers and Ralph Terry were spawned, and by the time Swango was finishing high school there were a dozen scouts in the stands every time he pitched. "They all wanted to fly me up to the big leagues for tryouts, but I didn't want to mess with that," he says. Eventually he signed with a fellow named Dutch Dietrich of the Baltimore Orioles.

What really happened at Baltimore? It could be there is a little truth from both sides. "Hell, he got so wild after a point," says one ex-Oriole who was there, another bonus baby named Jim Pyburn, "that we just refused to take batting practice against him." Swango says pitching coach Harry Brecheen tried to make him change everything he was doing, from his windup to his grip, and had him utterly confused after two weeks. "You can't believe how scared I was up there and how much I had to learn," he says. "One day I started pitching batting practice without a catcher. They had to tell me you don't never do that. Heck, I didn't know."

At any rate, two months after receiving his $36,000 and joining the Orioles, he was given his unconditional release. The newspapers were having fun with him, but when he got home to Oklahoma the next day he had calls from five scouts. "I kinda felt obligated to go back and sign with Richards if he wanted me, because of the money they'd give me, but my parents and my coach didn't think I should." He played occasional games with semipro teams here and there, and late in the summer signed with the New York Yankees organization.

He spent the next eight years in a frustrating odyssey through the minor leagues. In 1956 they tried him as an outfielder at McAlester, Oklahoma, in the Class D Sooner State League, where he hit only .240. From then on he was a pitcher. Greenville, Texas; Fargo, North Dakota; Greensboro, North Carolina; Amarillo.

Charlotte. Binghamton. Drafted from the Yankee organization after a good year at Nashville in 1961, he went to spring training with the Twins but he was sent out to Vancouver in Class AAA.

Swango's last year was 1963. He had a strong spring training and started out 2–2 with Dallas-Fort Worth. He thought he had found it, but then he was abruptly shipped out to Charlotte in the Sally League. "That kinda destroyed my confidence. I was twenty-six and I'd done a lot of traveling. I thought maybe it'd be better, you know, if I did something else." Minnesota asked him if he would be interested in going down to the winter instructional league during the off-season. "What do you want me to do," Swango asked them, "go down there and take care of them young boys for you?" It was over.

Not all of them went off to the big city as confused country boys, of course, although the majority of America's professional baseball players *have* come from small towns in the South and Midwest, and, recently, from California. One who was just as savvy as the next guy, and who kept up a running battle with organized baseball throughout his fiery ten-year career, is Frank Leja. Already six-foot-three and 210 pounds when he graduated from high school in Holyoke, Massachusetts, Leja was wanted so badly that three clubs were fined heavily by commissioner Ford Frick for holding secret tryouts before his American Legion season had ended. "That," says Leja, now an articulate man doing a booming insurance business in Nahant, Massachusetts, "is how my career began." Soon after blasting a 485-foot home run into the center-field bleachers at the old Polo Grounds during an intrasquad game, he signed with the Yankees for $50,000 during the World Series of 1953. Leja was seventeen years old.

Two decades later, his recollections have a vividness that comes only with pain. From the start, Leja felt put upon. When he checked into his first spring training, he found dollar signs, rather than his name, painted on every piece of equipment in his locker. The Yankee veterans—cold, proud defending world champions—treated him with icy contempt. During batting practice, when Leja inevitably popped the ball over the infield, manager

Casey Stengel would dip into his reservoir of sarcasm and wheeze: "*Look at that kid hit that ball!*" Coach Bill Dickey changed his entire batting stance, Leja says, and he never felt comfortable at the plate again.

Finally, when the season opened and he saw his first paycheck, Leja took on the baseball commissioner. "They were paying me based on *last* year's minimum for rookies," he recalls. "It's no big deal. I just thought I ought to get what was due to me. It was the principle of the thing." The buck passed all the way up to Commissioner Frick's office. "I was told to report there and right away I knew I was in trouble," Leja remembers. " 'Now what the hell is this about your salary?' Frick said to me, and when I tried to explain he cut me off. 'They gave you enough money,' he said. 'Now go on out there to the stadium and play ball!' "

During his enforced two years with the Yankees, Leja went to bat just seven times. He got one hit, was sent out to the minors and—except for a brief shot with the Angels in 1962 when he went hitless in sixteen trips—never came back. "You can't tell me baseball's not a family business," says Leja, still puzzled and angry at not being advanced during a sometimes dazzling eight-year career in the minors. "My composite totals for those eight years were 290 home runs, over 800 runs batted in and a .263 average, but every time I turned around I was being sent out to Amarillo. In '56 I'm at Binghamton for two months. I'm third in the league in home runs and second in runs batted in, hitting .240. So they tell me to go to Winston-Salem. Okay? You follow me?" The way Leja sees it, the Yankees' East Coast scout, Paul Krichell, the one who had originally signed him, died and the next day it was Winston-Salem for the rich kid who makes trouble.

The era of bonus babies is ancient history. The track record on young phenoms is so bad owners are no longer willing to gamble wildly. More important, all eligible amateurs are now placed in a free-agent draft, somewhat similar to the system in football and basketball, and can bargain with only one team at a time. And teams can no longer keep young players on ice in the minor leagues. Each winter, clubs are allowed to protect only forty men in their entire organization, on the big club and in the farm system, leaving all others open to a draft by other teams.

"Scouting's different now from what is was back then," says Mercer Harris, a Cardinals and Tigers scout in the Southeast for twenty-seven years. "The whole game's changing fast. Used to be, you'd find yourself a real *phee*-nom out in the country and keep him for yourself. It was a lot of fun. We didn't talk to each other any more than ballplayers stood around talking to the opposition at the batting cage. But you can't hide 'em now because of the draft and all." College baseball, in fact, could become the new minor leagues: a place where kids get educated, finish growing and play upwards of a hundred games a season under former major leaguers before moving straight into the big leagues. "Scouting was a lot more work then," says Harris, "but it was a lot more fun."

Astronomical bonuses didn't disappear completely after the mid-1950s, when the owners abandoned the "bonus rule" and the official bonus-baby era ended. Players like Rich Reichardt and Bob Bailey still signed six-figure contracts. But the $100,000 bonuses have now become a distinct rarity. Blue-chip prospects can still get bonuses, but the vast majority now are in the $30,000 range.

Mark Pettit got $30,000 from the Baltimore Orioles last year. He had to choose between going to college first or immediately going pro. His father called it "the biggest decision we as a family ever had to make." His father should know. In 1950, Paul Pettit was the first six-figure bonus baby, signing amid great fanfare with the Pittsburgh Pirates. Pettit was a monumental bust. Today, like so many of the original bonus babies, he is still trying to get over what happened to the dream, wondering where the money went, wishing he could have given it one more shot. Yet he was pleased that his son signed and chose to attend college only in the off-season. "If you play four years at Arizona State," Paul Pettit says, "you've still got to prove you can do it. They want to see if you can play pro ball."

When Paul Pettit signed with the Pirates for $100,000 in 1950 he was immediately sent to New Orleans in the tough Southern Association. "I think I could've become a good pitcher in the big leagues if I'd had a chance to come along slowly," he says. Instead, he hurt his arm that first year and pitched only thirty and two-thirds innings in the majors. Then came a decade all over the minors for him, later even a switch to first base in Class C.

Now he coaches baseball in the Los Angeles area, making a good living off that and rental property bought with his bonus, and says somewhat resignedly that he is "still plugging away." Sometimes, says his wife, "Lefty sort of drifts away into his own world, like nobody else is around." It seems to be a pattern. Do people still remember him? "Just the other day I went into a drugstore with a prescription and when the woman waiting on me saw the name she said, 'Aren't you a basketball player?' I said no, that I used to play *baseball*. They still get me confused with Bob Pettit, the basketball player."

The Rebels had beaten the Chiefs by one run, with the help of some late-inning maneuvering on the coach's part, and now the cool night air cloaked northeastern Oklahoma. Bruce Swango had rushed home, spent a few minutes taking needling from the kids about his crewcut, grabbed a bath and suited up to work at the tire plant all night. His wife had offered to run me up to Joplin so I could make my early morning flight, and after a detour to pick up her sister for company on the road back, we were out on the highway.

"I guess it's been pretty rough for you," I said.

"What?"

"The traveling and moving around."

"Oh," Joanne said, "you don't know the half of it. Remember the cattle he bought with some of his bonus money? Well, every time we ran out of money we'd just go out and sell another cow. They're all gone."

"I don't guess you miss that."

"No. I sure don't miss that part."

"How about Bruce?"

Joanne blinked her lights for a diesel to pass. "He doesn't sleep well sometimes," she said. "I don't know if it's what happened or what, but a lot of times he just sits and stares off somewhere. Oh, I'm sure he misses it. He wishes he'd kept on trying so he could prove himself. I feel bad about that. Maybe I should've talked him into playing longer. He only quit because of us."

"Us?"

"Me and the kids. He's a good man, a family man. He wants to move to a farm, and I think maybe that's what we should do. Move back to the farm. Then maybe he'll get it off his mind."

True, 1972

15

Yesterday's Hero

"A week never passes that the Alumni Office fails to receive news highlighting the good works of former football players. So many of them
reflect credit on our University."
—*University of Tennessee Football Guide,* 1970

What is fame?
An empty bubble;
Gold? A transient,
Shining trouble.
—James Grainger, 1721–1766

THE EVENING BEGAN WITH AN expedition to the friendly
neighborhood liquor store four blocks away, where a purchase of
four quarts of sticky-sweet Wild Irish Rose red wine was negoti-
ated with a reedy gray-haired man behind the cash register.
When the man saw who was shuffling through the front door his
jaw tightened and he glanced nervously around, as if checking to
be sure everything was nailed down.

"When you start drinking that stuff, Bob?" he asked.

"Since the last time I woke up and didn't know what month it
was," said Robert Lee Suffridge, inspiring a doleful exchange
about his drinking exploits. It was concluded that cheap wine at
least puts you to sleep before you have a chance to do something
crazy. Paying for the $1.39-a-quart bottles he trudged back out

the door into the dry late-afternoon July heat and nursed the bleached twelve-year-old Mercury back to his apartment.

It is an old folks' home, actually, a pair of matching six-story towers on the outskirts of Knoxville, Tennessee. At fifty-five he isn't ready for an old folks' home yet, but a brother who works for the state arranged for him to move in. Most of the other residents are well past the age of sixty-five, and to the older ladies like Bertha Colquitt, who lives in the apartment next to his and lets him use her telephone, he is their mischievous son. More than once they have had to call an ambulance for him when he was either drunk or having heart pains, but they don't seem to mind. "Honey, if I was about ten years younger you'd have to watch your step around me," he will say to one of them, setting off embarrassed giggles. God knows where he found four portable charcoal grills, but he keeps them in the dayroom downstairs and throws wiener roasts from time to time. He grows his own tomatoes beside his building, in a fiberglass crate filled with loam and human excrement taken from a buddy's septic tank.

Getting off the elevator at the fourth floor, he thumped across the antiseptic hallway. The cooking odors of cabbage and meat loaf and carrots drifted through doorways. Joking with an old woman walking down the hall with a cane, he shifted the sack of wine bottles to his left arm and opened the door to his efficiency apartment. A copy of *AA Today*, an Alcoholics Anonymous publication, rested atop the bureau. A powder-blue blazer with a patch reading "All-Time All-American" hung in a clear plastic bag from the closet doorknob. The bed, "my grandmother's old bed," had not been made in some time. Littering the living room floor were old sports pages and letters and newspaper clippings.

"Not a bad place," he said, filling a yellow plastic tumbler with wine and plopping down in the green Naugahyde sofa next to the wall. "Especially for forty-two-fifty a month."

"What's your income now?"

"About two hundred a month. Social Security, Navy pension."

"You don't need much, anyway, I guess."

He stood up and stepped to the picture window that looks out over the grassy courtyard separating the two buildings. In the harsh light he looked like the old actor Wallace Beery, with puffy broken face and watery eyes and rubbery lips, his shirttail hanging out over a bulging belly. "I'm an alcoholic," he said in a hoarse whisper. "I've done everything. Liquor, pills, everything. I don't even like the stuff. Never did like it, not even when I was playing ball. Hell, only reason I used to carry cigarettes was because my date might want a smoke." He drained the wine from the tumbler and turned away from the window, and there was no self-pity in his gravelly voice. "I came into the world a poor boy," he said, "and I guess I'm still a poor boy."

The 1970 Tennessee Football Guide was generally correct, of course, when it boasted about the steady flood of "news highlighting the good works of former football players." The good life awaits the young man who becomes a college football star. He gets an education, or at least a degree, whether he works at it or not. He becomes known and admired. He discovers the relationship between discipline and success. He makes connections with alumni in high places—men who, in their enthusiasm for football, cross his palm with money and create jobs for him. About all he has to do is mind his manners, do what he is told, and he will be presented with a magical key to an easy life after he is finished playing games. The rule applies to most sports. "If it hadn't been for baseball," a pint-sized minor-league outfielder named Ernie Oravetz once told me, "I'd be just like my old man today: blind and crippled from working in the mines up in Pennsylvania." For thousands of kids, particularly poor kids in the South, where football is a way of life, athletics has been a road out. Look at Jim Thorpe, the Native American. Look at Babe Ruth, the orphan. Look at Willie Mays, the black man. Look at Joe Namath.

But look, also, at the ones who couldn't make it beyond the last hurrah. Look at Carl Furillo and Joe Louis and the others— the ones who died young, the ones who blew their money, the ones who ruined their bodies, the ones who somehow missed the brass ring. Fame is an empty bubble, indeed, easily burst if not handled with care. What happens when the legs go, the arm tires, the eyes fade, the lungs sag? Some cope, some don't. The reasons some don't are so varied and sometimes so subtle they require the attention of sociologists. But the failures are there, and they will always be with us.

Few bubbles have burst quite so dramatically as that of Bob Suffridge. A runaway who had been scratching out his own living in the streets of Knoxville since the age of 15, Suffridge went on to be named one of the eleven best college football players of all time. He weighed only 185 pounds, but he had killer instincts and rabbit quickness and the stamina of a mule. "He was so quick, he could get around you before you got off your haunches," says one former teammate. "Suff was the archetype of the Tennessee single-wing pulling guard," says his friend and Knoxville *Journal* sports columnist Tom Anderson. Playing both ways for coach Bob Neyland, averaging more than fifty minutes a game, Suffridge was in on the beginning of a dynasty that became one of the strongest traditions in American college football: the Tennessee Volunteers, the awesome single-wing offense, "The Big Orange," those lean and fast and hungry shock troops of "the General." During three seasons at UT, 1938–40, Suffridge never played in a losing regular-season game (though the Vols did lose two of three bowl games, the first of many postseason appearances for the school). He was everybody's All-American in 1938 and 1940 and made some teams in 1939. In 1961 he was named to the national football Hall of Fame, and during college football's centennial celebration two years ago joined the company of such men as Red Grange and Jim Thorpe and Bronko Nagurski on the eleven-man All-Time All-American team. "Bob," says George Cafego, a Vol tailback then and a UT assistant coach now, "had every opportunity to be a millionaire."

There may be no millionaires among the Vols of that era, but there are few slackers. The late Bowden Wyatt was head coach of the Vols for eight seasons. Ed Molinski is a doctor in Memphis. Ed Cifers is president of a textile company. Abe Shires is a sales coordinator for McKesson-Robbins. Bob Woodruff is the UT athletic director.

All of which makes Suffridge an even sadder apparition as he drifts in and out of Knoxville society today, an aimless shadow of the hyped-up kid who used to blitz openings for George Cafego and who once blocked three consecutive Sammy Baugh punt attempts in a brief fling with the pros. Over the past twenty-five years he has tried working—college coaching, selling insurance, hawking used cars, promoting Coca-Cola, running for public office, and running a liquor store (in that order)—but something would always happen. He hasn't worked now in about five years. He has had two heart attacks, one of them laying him up for eight months. He has engaged in numerous battles with booze, winning some and losing others. He has gone through and survived a period with pills. Now a bloated 250 pounds, he lives alone at the Cagle Terrace Apartments (he lost his wife and four kids to divorce twelve years ago, although now and then one of the children will come to see him), where he seems to have made a separate peace with the world. He made the local papers recently by protesting when two armed guards showed up to supervise a July 4 party there. ("Bob Suffridge, a former All-American football player at Tennessee, complained that elderly residents were frightened at the sudden appearance of the men with guns. . . . Suffridge serves on a committee to help set up socials for elderly residents and also lives at Cagle Terrace.") He spends his time hanging around the sports department of the Knoxville *Journal,* going fishing with buddy Tom Anderson, writing spontaneous letters to people like Paul ("Bear") Bryant, talking old times with Cafego and publicist Haywood Harris at UT's shimmering new athletic plant, and sitting for hours in such haunts as Dick Comer's Sports Center (a pool hall) and Polly's Tavern and Tommy Ford's South Knoxville American Legion Club No. 138.

Except for a handful of sympathetic acquaintances, some of whom have battled booze themselves, Knoxville doesn't really seem to care much about him anymore. When a woman in the upper-class suburbs heard a magazine was planning a story on Suffridge, she said only, in a low gasp, *"Oh, my God."* There is a great deal of embarrassment on the part of the university, although officials there recognize an obligation to him and have, over the years, with fingers crossed, invited him to appear at banquets and halftime ceremonies. "It's really pretty pitiful," says another Knoxvillian. The newspapers generally treat him gently— "He is now a Knoxville businessman," the *Journal* said after his Hall of Fame selection in 1961—and mercifully let it go at that.

Even when you talk to those who know him best you get little insight into what when wrong. Says Tom Anderson: "He's smarter than you'd think he is, and I thought for a while he was going to straighten up. But I guess you have to regard him as a great athlete who never grew up. It gets worse when he starts talking about the old days. He can get to crying in a minute. Some of those big guys are like that." George Cafego is clearly puzzled by it all: "I don't believe the guy's allergic to work. I've *seen* him work." Ben Byrd of the *Journal* paints a picture of a man who has always marched to a different drummer: "He used to drive into town, park his car anywhere he felt like it, pull up the hood like he had engine trouble, and be gone all day. That time Coke hired him to do PR, he got fired when they had a big board meeting and he put a tack on the chair of the chairman of the board. He doesn't mean to cause trouble. Maybe he just never understands the situation. I mean, like when he was sergeant-at-arms for the state legislature one time and didn't like the way a debate was going, he demanded the floor."

Perhaps the best friend Suffridge has is a lanky Knoxville attorney named Charlie Burks, a friend from college days who is a recovering alcoholic himself and deserves some credit for the occasions when Suffridge is in control of things. "Oh, Bob's a great practical joker all right," says Burks. "But what do you say about him and his troubles? He's looking for something, but he doesn't know what it is."

There was a time many years ago when Bob Suffridge knew exactly what he was looking for: three square meals a day and a place to sleep at night. He was born in 1916 on a farm in Raccoon Valley, then a notorious hideout for bootleggers, situated some twenty miles from Knoxville. As one of seven children he often had to help his father carry sacks of sugar and stoke the fire for a moonshine still, but that didn't last long. Bob wanted to go to school and play football, against his father's wishes, and one day when he was fifteen there was a big fight between the two and Bob left home. He wandered into Fountain City, a suburb of Knoxville, where he fended for himself.

"I was living on a park bench at first," he recalls. "One day I went into this doctor's office and got a job going in early in the morning to sweep out the building and start the fire, for two dollars and fifty cents a week. I noticed they had some bedsprings next to the heater in the basement—no mattress, just springs— and since I had a key to the place I started sleeping there." The doctor, a Dr. Carl Martin, came in unusually early one morning on an emergency call and found Suffridge asleep in his clothes and saw that he got a mattress and some blankets. Soon another doctor hired him to clean up his office, too, meaning an additional $2.50 a week. "For two years I lived like that. I carried newspapers, worked in a factory, cleaned out those offices and even joined the National Guard so I could pick up another twelve dollars every three months. I didn't go hungry. I was a monitor at school, and took to stealing my lunch out of lockers."

In the meantime, he was asserting himself as the football star with the Central High School Bobcats. "Maybe I was hungrier than the rest of them," he says. He was almost fully developed physically at the age of eighteen, an eager kid with tremendous speed and reflexes, and in 1936 he captained the Bobcats to the Southern high school championship. Central won thirty-three consecutive games, and Suffridge became a plum for the college recruiters.

Tennessee was the school he wanted. "They already had a lot of tradition. Everybody wanted to play for General Neyland." Something of a loner, a poor country boy accustomed to fighting solitary battles, he spent every ounce of his energy on the football field. "I couldn't get along with anybody. I couldn't understand them." Although he and Neyland were always at odds, there was a curious, if unspoken, mutual respect between the nail-hard disciplinarian and his moody, antagonistic little guard.

Once the last cheers of the 1940 season had died, Bob Suffridge appeared to have the world in his hands. He earned a degree in physical education ("I guess I thought maybe I'd be a coach one day"), married a UT coed and signed to play with the Philadelphia Eagles. He was named All-Pro for the 1941 season, but more important than that was what happened in the last regular game of the year. It was played on Sunday, December 7. "That was the day I blocked three of Sammy Baugh's punts," he says, "but nobody paid any attention the next day. At halftime somebody had come into the dressing room and told us Pearl Harbor had been bombed by the Japs. I'd have been the hero of the day except for that." Suffridge immediately joined the Navy.

In retrospect, that announcement of the attack on Pearl Harbor was the pivotal moment in Suffridge's life. As executive officer on a troop attack transport, he suffered only a slight shrapnel wound to his right leg and went through no especially traumatic experiences. What hurt was the timing of it all. He was twenty-five and in peak physical condition when he went in, but a flabby thirty when he came out. He tried to make a comeback with the Eagles during the 1946 season, but he weighed 225 and was soon riding the bench. The bubble had burst, and he was confused. There would be occasional periods of promise, but once the 1950s came it was a steady, painful downhill slide.

Giving up on pro football, he tried college coaching—at North Carolina State under ex-Vol great Beattie Feathers, and at the Citadel under his old high school coach, Quinn Decker. Next he went to work as an insurance agent for a company in Knoxville, and after three good years he decided to open his own agency. The business did all right for a while, thanks to his name and his contacts around town, but he started in on the pills and the booze and soon had to unload it. ("I sold out for a good profit," Suffridge says, but others say the business fell flat.) And then the wandering began. He went to Nashville to sell used cars. He blew the public relations job with Coca-Cola. He was divorced by his wife in March of 1960, a year before his election to the football Hall of Fame. The chronology of his life became a blur after that. He ran for clerk of the Knox County court and nearly defeated a man who was considered one of the strongest politicians around and who later became mayor of Knoxville. He had to be literally propped up, to the horror of UT officials, at numerous occasions when he was being paraded around as the Vols' greatest player. He drifted to Atlanta, where, for a year, he drank more than he sold at a friend's liquor store. He worked briefly for the state highway department. Finally, around 1965, shortly after the private publication of a boozy paperback biography entitled *Football Beyond Coaching*—compiled in various taverns by Suffridge and a local sportswriter known as Raymond ("Streetcar") Edmunds—he suffered two heart attacks.

"Yeah, me and Streetcar had a lot of fun with that book," Suffridge was saying. It was almost dark now, and we had driven out to Tommy Ford's American Legion club. This is the place where Suffridge's Hall of Fame plaque had hung majestically behind the bar for several months before outraged UT officials finally got it for display in a glass showcase on campus, and the place where Suffridge has spent many a night locked up without anybody knowing he was there. He was saying farewell to his friends, for in the morning he would leave for a month's vacation at Daytona Beach as the guest, or mascot, of his attorney friend Charlie Burks and a doctor from Jamestown, Tennessee. He had dropped a couple of dollars at the nickel slot machine and now he was sitting at the bar, playing some sort of game of chance for a bottle of bourbon.

"How'd the book do?" somebody asked.

"Damn best-seller," he said. "Hell, I made about seventeen thousand dollars off that thing. Sold it for two bucks. We'd have done better than that if we hadn't given away so many. I'd load a batch in the trunk of my car and head out for Nashville, Memphis, and Chattanooga. Sell 'em to people I knew at stores and in bars. Then I'd come back home and find Streetcar sitting in Polly's Tavern and I'd ask him how many he'd sold while I was gone and he'd say he'd gotten rid of two hundred. 'Well, where's the money?' I'd ask him, and he'd say he gave 'em away. Street was almost as good a businessman as I was."

"Go on, Bob, take another chance," said a blonde named Faye.

"Another? Honey, that's getting to be expensive liquor."

"Price of liquor never seemed to bother you much."

"Guess you're right about that." A phone rang. "Get that, will you?" he said. "Might be somebody."

And so it goes, an evening with Bob Suffridge. They are all like that, they say: aimless hours of puns and harmless practical jokes and, if the hour is late enough and the pile of beer cans high enough, those infinitely sad moments when his eyes water up as he talks on about the missed opportunities and the wasted years. How can anyone pass judgment, though, without having come through the same pressures he has? *I came into the world a poor boy, and I'm still a poor boy.* What a man has to do is be grateful for the good times and try to live with the bad.

We were finishing steaks at a motel dining room, washing them down with beer, when the waitress could stand it no longer. A well-preserved woman near Suffridge's age, she had been stealing glances at him throughout the meal. She finally worked up her nerve as she was clearing the table, turning to me and saying with an embarrassed grin: "Excuse me, but didn't I hear you call him Bob?"

"That's right."

"Well, I thought so." For the first time she looked directly at Suffridge. "You're Bob Suffridge, aren't you?"

He wiped his mouth and said, "I guess I am."

"I was Penny Owens. I went to Central High with you."

"Penny . . . ?"

"Oh, you wouldn't remember me. You never would even look at me twice when we were in school."

They talked for a few minutes about old times and former classmates. There was an awkward silence. "So," she said, "ah, what are you *doing* now, Bob?"

"Nothing."

She flushed. "Oh."

He suppressed a belch and then looked up at her with a mischievous grin. "You want to help me?"

"Aw, you."

"Awww, you."

Sport, 1972

Epilogue

So where are they now, these men and women who shared a glimpse of their lives with me so many years ago? Karl Wallenda died as he would have wanted it, five years after our meeting: with a huge crowd gawking from the streets below in San Juan, Puerto Rico, holding its collective breath as he attempted to walk the wire between two skyscrapers in a promotional gig, they gasped to see him lose his balance in a crosswind and fall to his death. Ty Cobb, alone and rich and bitter, passed peacefully in 1960 in a hospital bed in his hometown of Royston, Georgia, prompting as many stories about his riotous life and general meanness as about his greatness as "the Georgia Peach." Poor Bob Suffridge went quietly, as well, dying in that nursing home in Knoxville soon after I met him; sober too late, ashes to ashes.

Marty Malloy and I spent many hours together during the mid-1990s as I tracked him for a book about a kid working his way up through the minor leagues. *The Heart of the Game* focused on Marty's 1994 season with the Durham Bulls, and even after its publication I kept up with him as he advanced, step by step, ever closer to the majors. I was sitting in front of the television set one Saturday in early September of '98 at my home in Atlanta when the phone rang. It was one of the Braves' beat writers, a friend, calling from the press box at Shea Stadium: "The kid just checked in and he's hitting in the two-hole." Marty homered into the Mets' bullpen that day, in his first major-league game, and I was taking so many phone calls that you would've thought he was my own son. He since has been released by the Braves, but keeps having such strong seasons in Triple-A that he's still plugging away at the age of thirty.

Gene Asher has been a friend for decades, and we see each other often, but he quit going to Braves games when salaries zoomed out of sight in the '90s, preferring to remember the game when it was simpler, when Charlie Glock played third base and Gene was a peanut vendor for the Atlanta Crackers. I know little about any of the others in this collection. The roller derby is gone, as far as I know; and the suffering of the boys at Stalag Thirteen in Charleston, West Virginia, ended soon after my visit when their jackleg semi-pro football league went under. The Birmingham Barons play in a modern ballpark in the distant suburbs, but once each summer they draw around ten thousand fans for an official Southern League game at old Rickwood Field to ensure its status as one of the oldest "active" parks in America. Being an Auburn alumnus in good standing, I still run into the boys of the '57 National Champions, a true brotherhood, they hailing me as "Scoop!" when they see me, just like the old days. And Dixie Speedway is still thriving, a joyful alternative to the commercially-oriented Winston Cup tracks in the South, a place I visit at least once each season. The fictional "Stud Cantrell" and his girlfriend, "Dixie Lee Box," had an afterlife of sorts when HBO filmed my novel, *Long Gone,* roundly hailed by the New York Times and recently deemed by *Newsday* "one of the best sports movies ever made."

It was soon after the release of *Long Gone,* in fact, that I came across two men who had figured in my life while my dreams of playing professional baseball were still alive: Spencer ("Onion") Davis and Roy Sinquefield, neither of whom would have ever heard of me if I hadn't written about them. I was giving a speech one day in Americus, Georgia, when my host told me that the great Onion Davis was retiring that very day as the county's school superintendent, a shadow of the lefty with the wicked curveball he had been in the 1950s, and when I found him cleaning out his office I could think of only one thing to say: "Better we meet here, in our old age, than at sixty feet, six inches."

Sinquefield, the manager who had fired me from the Panama City Flyers in 1954, dropped me a letter after the publication of the novel in '79: "Apparently, letting you go wasn't the only mistake I made, because they fired me six weeks later. Anyway, I'd always wanted to be a long-distance trucker, just like your daddy, and I thought you'd like to know my CB handle. It's 'Long Gone.'" That seemed to bring everything full circle for me, the kid who became a writer when he found he could neither hit nor turn the double play.

About the Author

Veteran writer Paul Hemphill, the author of fifteen books, including *Leaving Birmingham: Notes of a Native Son* and *The Ballad of Little River,* has focused much of his writing career on the blue-collar South. In addition to writing about a racially inspired church arson in rural Alabama, growing up in a hostile and racially conflicted Birmingham, and chronicling the rise of "the Nashville sound" and the culture it produced, Hemphill got his start as a sports writer, training that served as a foundation for much of what he would later write. Hemphill has spent decades writing about sports on and off for daily newspapers and national magazines.